DOES MY BUM LOOK BIG IN THIS?

Kristin,

Just a little something to read on the plane and hopefully also a reminder of a friend who asks herself this really every day

Nick,
xxx

.50
8/21

About the author

Arabella Weir is a writer and performer who started her career as the gladioli wiper for Dame Edna Everage. She appears regularly on television in various guises – in all of Alexei Sayle's TV series, *Harry Enfield & Chums* and *The Lenny Henry Show.* She is one of the regular cast of *The Fast Show,* for which she writes and performs 'Different with Boys' and 'Insecure Woman', among others. Arabella has spent her life on the run from her bottom but now it pays for its upkeep. This is her first book, so if you don't like it, don't tell her – and if you do like it, she won't believe you.

Does My Bum Look Big In This?

The Diary of an Insecure Woman

Arabella Weir

CORONET BOOKS
Hodder and Stoughton

Copyright © Arabella Weir 1997

First published in Great Britain in 1997 by Hodder and Stoughton
A division of Hodder Headline PLC
First published in paperback in 1998 by Hodder and Stoughton
A Coronet paperback

10 9 8 7 6 5 4

A CIP catalogue record for this title is available from
the British Library

ISBN 0 340 68948 X

Printed and bound in Great Britain by
Clays Ltd, St Ives plc

Hodder and Stoughton
A division of Hodder Headline PLC
338 Euston Road
London NW1 3BH

For my Mum and Dad –
without whom this would not have been possible.

ACKNOWLEDGMENTS

Whilst writing this book I had much encouragement and support from many people, but in particular I would like to thank: Jon Canter, Charlie Higson, Paul Whitehouse, Helen Scott-Lidgett, Betsy Blair Reisz, David Tennant, Sue Andrew, Tracy Hargreaves, Simon Prosser, Anna-Maria Watters, Sarah Lutyens and Jeremy Norton.

Jacqueline M. Pane ... I'm not saying what the M stands for ... anyway it's not important. I just use it because it makes my name sound better and more interesting, OK?

Address: Flat B, 17 Saint Bartholomews Road, London, NW6. Look, if you're returning this to my home address and it's during the day, I'll be at work, so try the bell for Flat C, Mrs Mellish, the old lady who lives across the hall from me. She's very deaf, but keep trying, she'll definitely be in – she's housebound. If you don't get an answer from her and you can hear *Coronation Street* then she's got the telly turned up so loud you might as well give up. Anyway, on no account give it to Downstairs Man, the bloke who lives in Flat A, on the ground floor. Even if he's in *DO NOT GIVE HIM THIS DIARY*, it's got things about him and his loud sex life in it, I'd have to sell my flat if he saw this – so please, please don't give it to him, even as a joke.

You *could* drop it in to my work, The Pellet Corporation, 130 The Strand, London, WC2. But absolutely do not leave it with the Conference Department secretary – New Secretary Sarah, she's far too pleasant and over-confident for my liking. I've got nothing concrete against her yet but she laughed at a joke I made the other day, so there must be *something* wrong with her. I don't want to see a knowing smirk on her lips as she hands over my lost diary – 'This was dropped off for you, Ms Pane.' Best thing would be if you asked to see the Senior Conference Organiser – that's me. By the way, although my job title says Senior, it isn't as grand as it sounds. There's only three of us in the department and I've been there the longest, so they kind of had to make me the Senior one, it's not because I'm great or important or anything. I've just thought, it's not Senior because I'm close to retirement age either, I don't think it means Senior as in old ... God, maybe it does and that's why they gave me the title ...

Anyway, look, on second thoughts, I'd rather not see you face to face if you've read any of this diary, so could you just ask for ... erm ... Clare in New Accounts ... no ... can't trust her, she's too thin ... erm ... WHAT ON EARTH AM I THINKING OF?? Forget everything I've said, just put it into a heavily sealed envelope, use gaffer tape – it's impossible to steam off – and leave it (only if you can't get to my house) at the main reception, write on the envelope that it's very urgent and confidential. Also, by the way, wrap it in some newspaper or tissue or something, otherwise someone might notice that the packet is diary-shaped and cotton on. Look, on second thoughts, I'll just spend the rest of my life looking at strangers on the bus and thinking 'Is it you? Are you the one that has read my innermost thoughts? Are you giving me a funny look because you've read my diary and think I'm pathetic?' so just burn it, OK?

IN CASE OF EMERGENCY CONTACT:

Mrs Sheila Pane (they divorced six years ago but she still calls herself Mrs)

Swallow's Flight (not my idea, I can assure you)
Birch Hollow
Warwickshire

This is my mum – for the love of God, don't contact her unless it really is an emergency, otherwise I'll never hear the end of it.

OR

Ralph Pane
31 Priory Mansions
MacIntosh Road
London SW6

Looks like a posh address, I know, but you can't swing a cat in there. They are looking for a house abroad at the moment but meanwhile my Dad's wife, Jennifer, insists they live within a four-pound taxi-ride radius of Harvey Nichols. By the way, unless you have a death wish, if you find this diary, do not give it to my stepmother.

3 January

Hello! . . . Jacqueline Pane here, single, age . . . erm . . . ah . . . erm . . . 31 . . . OK, alright then, 33. I'm 5′ 5″, size 12 . . . well, actually the thing is I *can* just about fit into a size 12 but only if it's not really tight . . . otherwise it would probably be more honest to say size 14. Well, my top half's a size 12 (or 14 if it's from Next) and my bottom half is usually a size 14 – but definitely not bigger. Admittedly it was a size 16 the other day but that was at M&S and they've obviously changed the people that cut their clothes or something because I've *always* been able to get into their size 14, so I don't know what was going on with those trousers, maybe they'd been made in a foreign country where everyone's small . . . where are pygmies from? Anyway, let's just say size 12 to 14, on a bad day, OK? My friends call me Jackie and my family call me Jack, which I hate, so that's probably why they do it. People at work mostly seem to call me Jacqueline – don't know why they don't use the more familiar-sounding Jackie . . . they probably think I'm too forbidding or something for that, or perhaps they just don't want to be over-friendly in case I think they want to be friends outside work. My best friend Sally calls me Queline most of the time, I sort of like that because it sounds grown-up and glamorous, not all butch like Jack. Actually, I've never written Queline down before, I don't think it reads well, it looks like a cream you use to get rid of thrush. Must make sure Sally never addresses a card to me as that. So here I am, I live alone in a nice (– ish, I mean it was all I could afford but ideally I'd like something bigger) one-bedroom flat in Queen's Park. It's nowhere near a park, of course, it's just some made-up name to make a not very posh area sound posh. I am the Senior Conference Organiser for The Pellet Corporation, the largest computer and parts supplier in England (does that include Scotland or doesn't it matter?). By the way, about being single, I am now, but only since last July. It's not that I was married until last July but I was sort of engaged. OK, strictly speaking, not actually engaged officially, properly, it's just that I had sort of assumed that as Perfect Peter and I had been together for a bit over a year . . . you know, you kind of think maybe, probably, but I was wrong. I mean I know he never proposed but I stupidly thought there was a chance it might be on the cards . . . anyway I couldn't have been more wrong. Turns out the only things on *his* cards were dumping me and taking up a job offer in New York, all at the same time.

Oh, wait a minute, you don't say 'hello' in your diary, like you're talking to someone else, and what am I doing introducing myself? Typical – I don't even know how to start a diary. Anyway, new diary, new life. Right. I know I've started this a bit late – I meant to start it on 1 January – like a normal person would. I mean if you are starting a diary you do it on the first day of the year, don't you? Thing is, I lost my new diary on 31 December and didn't manage to get another one until today. I bought it from the same shop I'd got the first one and even though I wore a hat, I could tell the shop assistant recognised me and was thinking 'Lost the first one you bought, eh? I'll bet you're not very good at your job, if you can't even hold on to a poxy new diary for a few days.'

I'm starting afresh. I'm going to have a more positive attitude to life. Yeah, I'm going to stop beating myself up about every little thing. Oh, help, I'm tempting fate now – God'll really punish me for this and probably organise it for me to get the sack when I go back to work, or have a permanently maiming accident, or be given a seat on the bus by a young person or something awful.

Erm . . . not doing well on my new positive attitude. Sorry . . . who am I saying sorry to? Fabulous, now I'm apologising to myself.

Anyway, right, I suppose I'd better have some New Year's resolutions, hadn't I? That is what you do, isn't it, when you start a diary . . . don't you? You write down all the good things you are going to do. Yeah, right, so that two months later, they're there as a glaring reminder of how bad you are at keeping even your own personal resolutions . . . oh, I might as well write some anyway.

10 NEW YEAR'S RESOLUTIONS

1. Start really thinking ahead. When you get dressed or do a project at work . . . in fact when you do anything at all from now on, always think of *any* area someone might criticise and then either criticise it first or pretend it was a mistake.
2. Be thinner.
3. Be better at everything.
4. Be grateful for most men's attention (obviously that doesn't include the *really* awful ones, unless they are *very* keen).
5. Do not have too much to drink at Christmas or parties and start feeling depressed about Perfect Peter again.
6. Start and do not break new, all-important Chinese macrobiotic/starvation diet thing – being thin *will* change your life.
7. Make a lot of money on the side by writing one of

those self-help books, like the ones I've got loads of.

8. Make up a very confident pseudonym for self-help book, the sort of name that combined with the title gives the reader the impression that your life is fantastic in every possible way and that theirs is shit.

9. Can't think of any more ... what does that say about me? I can't even think of ten resolutions ... oh, maybe it doesn't have to be ten.

5 January

Back to work. Feeling much better, haven't eaten for three days now – great! Fainted when I went to the lavatory but only for a couple of seconds. Decided I could face the world now that I'm a fraction thinner ... bit of a delay doing this, suddenly realised how desperate and keen I looked in those earrings with the dangly bits that I'd thought were sort of young and trendy. How wrong can you be? The newspaper bloke was looking for some change when I suddenly realised what he was really thinking – 'Don't you think you're a bit old for high-fashion earrings?' I grabbed my paper then quickly ducked down an alley so that I could root about in the bottom of my handbag undetected – found a pair of silver studs and put them on immediately. Then I looked like an extra from *Prisoner Cell Block H* – a stroppy, dumpy woman of indeterminate sexuality. Still, that was better than looking like I thought I was young and attractive.

Leaving work, I saw Attractive New Andy from Marketing. I bumped into him in the lift, he did smile at me but I'm absolutely sure he moved to make room for me when I got in, like he was thinking, 'Oh, she's quite fat, I'll have to move right over to the other side.' He did actually suggest we had a drink together some time but I'm sure that's because he felt guilty about having moved to make room for me and realised that I knew this was because he thought I was fat. Perhaps I'm being a bit silly – maybe he just wants to have a drink with me because he feels sorry for me and thinks I've got no friends. Yeah, maybe that's all it is.

6 January

Not a bad day at work, completely cleared my desk of all the backlog of papers from the Crowley job which was good, because it meant I was sitting down all day and I didn't have to worry about Andy seeing how big my bum is and changing his mind about that drink.

Probably shouldn't have worn that red suit though because Bossy Bowyer from the Senior Management team said something about how well organised the Christmas party was, as he passed me in the hall. I didn't have anything to do with organising it! He must have been thinking, 'She'd have made a hilarious Father Christmas in that suit.' Why else would he have mentioned it? Oh, great, just realised he'd probably noticed the beard I've sprouted thanks to my current bout of PMT, and thought that would have made me an extra-specially amusing and appropriate Father Christmas.

8 January

Went to the sales, gave up after two shops. Everywhere I went I knew the assistants were thinking, 'Oh, please, why are you bothering to spend money on clothes, tents from Milletts would be more suitable.'

9 January

Woke up feeling like a complete fool. Why, oh, why did I buy those platforms? I thought they looked alright when I tried them on but now I realise that girl in the shop was really thinking I looked like a hippopotamus in orthopaedic shoes. Of course, she was right.

10 January

Six Ryvitas, half a teaspoon of no-fat, no-flavour cottage cheese and two wrinkled tangerines since Saturday and several gallons of that Chinese macrobiotic tea. It tastes a lot like lavatory cleaner with old coins soaked in it – must be really good for you. Feel great. The smoking really helps. It's probably easier to keep eating like this if I can get really properly addicted to fags.

NB: just realised that cigarettes are a brilliant substitute for food.

Anyway, things were beginning to look up once I'd got the nicotine stains off my teeth ... well, most of them, I'll do the rest tomorrow, I've done the ones you see if I smile (just must remember not to smile properly until I've done the bottom ones), so I settled down to watch *E.R.* and they'd replaced it with some pathetic documentary about anorexics – like I should feel sorry for *them*. So, pissed off, I ate a slice of bread and butter – oh God, when will it ever change?

Same day, 2 a.m. – I'm now lying in bed, can't face my usual middle-of-the-night weigh-in, I just know I've put on at least half a pound. The bus conductor's going to notice and give me a pitying look, sort of saying, 'Well, hello, Miss Piggy, how do you expect to get a seat on the bus with that fat arse?' It's one of those pay-as-you-enter buses but all the same he's definitely going to be thinking that as he looks at me in his rear-view mirror.

Decided to weigh myself after all – and thanks a lot, God – weighed another pound. Went back to bed. No point going to work if everyone is going to laugh at me.

11 January

Had to go into work today. Bossy Bowyer phoned and said they couldn't manage without me, so unless I was really ill could I please try and come in. Don't know who he thinks he's fooling with that 'Can't manage without you, Jacqueline, you're the only one who can handle the bigger clients and your presence is vital in the office' ... Yeah, right, vital to give everyone else a laugh when they see how fat I've got and laugh at me when I go to the coffee machine, or maybe he means vital because I probably make everybody else look good because I'm so useless. Oh, dear me, I'm being very negative, aren't I? Maybe I'm vital because I'm good at my job ... feels weird writing something like that down, hope God doesn't read this and pay me back.

14 January

Haven't had time to write for a couple of days, been completely rushed off my feet at work. Wasn't really ill I suppose anyway, just a bit overweight and that's not, strictly speaking, ill ... is it? Things are really hotting up at work. There's this big new client, Pozzi Software, they are an Italian company and have been exporting new software to Britain for a year and now they want to set up a couple of conferences, half as a sort of thank you to their sales reps and half to promote the new stuff they've got. Should be quite fun to do because they want the conferences to have an Italian theme ... Italian catering, Italian music ... I've just had a thought. Aren't all Italian women fat? What if Bossy Bowyer wants me to handle this job because he thinks the clients will feel at home with me because I look like some sort of Italian mama. I was wearing that printed floral dress the day we discussed this brief – Bossy Bowyer probably thought it was an apron. I suppose I might have got the job because I can speak some Italian but I'll bet it's the fat bum and the apron really.

15 January

Great news. Attractive New Andy from Marketing is handling the Pozzi account, he came over this morning and told me. One thing, though. He said, 'It'll give us an excuse to have that drink now' ... what does he mean excuse, why does he need an excuse? Is he married? Does he live with his mum? Is he in the army? Why would he say 'excuse'? I don't feel comfortable about that word – maybe he sees having a drink with me as a kind of last resort, the sort of thing you would only do as a way of getting out of something *really* onerous like football practice. Marvellous, so I'm the sort of sick note of dating, am I? He did say 'give *us* an excuse' ... oh, maybe he was flirting. I wouldn't know flirtatious banter from a bar of soap, so I can't decide whether it was flirting or letting me know that if we ever actually have a relationship (hah!) then he'll always need an 'excuse' to be with me.

NB: Honestly, I've just reread that bit. From now, I *must not* analyse every single word someone I like says to me ... well, it does sort of help clarify things before you get too ... no, that's it, no more scrutinising another person's every word and gesture ... the thing is it can be very revealing and sort of helpful ... no, no, no, this must end, do not scrutinise every possible meaning of every little word ... OK, that's it, I won't, from now on, I will let things pass ... well, what about just every sentence instead ... that wouldn't be as bad, would it? Right ... just 'excuse', then ...

16 January

Not such great news. Thin Clare from New Accounts is also handling the Pozzi job – now I've got no chance with ANA (new abbreviation for Attractive New Andy, I'm getting bored with having to write that out every time ... only problem with this abbreviation is that if anyone ever reads this diary and doesn't see what ANA stands for they'll probably think I'm a lesbian – terrific). At lunchtime, in the canteen, Thin Clare was behind me in the queue, so I deliberately only had a fizzy water and a couple of crackers with nothing on them – that'll show her. Anyway, she sat at the same table as me and said she was very pleased to be having this opportunity to work with me ... I wonder what she meant by that? She also told me she'd recently got engaged to her childhood sweetheart, Paul. Sort of felt relieved for a minute, you know, because of ANA and everything, then I realised that blokes always seem to like girls they can't have, so it'll only make ANA keener on her, assuming he likes her at all which I don't know, of course, but it's always best to assume the worst. Really, I must stop this, it's very nice that Thin Clare is getting engaged ... I wonder if Paul is thin too? Lucky Clare – *really* thin and engaged.

Got home late and realised I hadn't eaten anything all day apart from that fizzy water and the crackers, feel a bit light-headed ... great, probably losing weight even as I'm writing this. Oh, I did eat a couple of those wonderful Pret à Manger Chunky Chicken, Walnut, Dolcelatte and Extra

Mayonnaise sandwiches when I popped out earlier, but I was walking when I ate them so they don't *really* count, do they? I'm sure food consumed when you are in motion has no calorific value – in real terms, does it?

NB: Important meeting re Pozzi account not till 10 a.m., so I can have a little lie-in before starting to get ready, set clock for 5.30 a.m.

17 January

I'd allowed three and a half hours to get dressed, luckily it was just about enough. This morning me, ANA, Thin Clare and Bossy Bowyer are meeting with Carlo Pozzi of Pozzi Software to go through ideas etc. for the conferences. Obviously I need to look my absolute best as ANA is going to be in there and the only way to get to the coffee percolator involves having to turn my back to the table . . . I suppose I could call someone in to do it for me but that might look a bit lazy.

Decided to wear my lilac jacket with the long black skirt, they aren't really supposed to go together and actually they do look a bit odd as an ensemble. Thing is, the jacket is the best one for sitting down in and the skirt makes my bum look marginally slimmer. Anyway, I'll stay sat down once the meeting's over while everyone is leaving . . . like I'm writing notes or something.

10 p.m. – exhausted but had to write about the meeting. It went really well, I managed to stay seated the entire time and Thin Clare poured the coffee before I'd even had time to start panicking about getting up. Oh yeah, *and* the client seemed to like my ideas for the conferences as well. Carlo Pozzi was

very good-looking, about 35 years old or so, speaks beautiful English with a sort of foreign accent (obviously) and he kept staring at me and every time I told him about one of the ideas he'd say it was great. I was a bit puzzled by that until it dawned on me that he obviously fancied Thin Clare and must have been trying to make her jealous by pretending he found me attractive and interesting. Don't know what was wrong with ANA, he seemed a bit sulky. Perhaps he hates lilac.

25 January

Really sorry haven't written anything for ages. Things have been really hectic at the office and at home. It looks like somebody has bought the flat downstairs but more about that later. I've spent the last week trying to put together a plan of action for the series of conferences Carlo Pozzi has now decided he wants rather than the two originally planned. He rings me practically every day to go over things and discuss plans . . . great, it must be because he thinks I need constant monitoring – can't think why else he's always on the phone. Mind you, he doesn't often ask about the conferences, sometimes he just rings and never mentions the work . . . oh, I've just realised, I bet he makes sure that our receptionist mentions to Thin Clare that he rings me a lot – clever work. I expect his plan is to make Thin Clare really jealous before he approaches her . . . funnily enough, I don't think he has ever spoken to her, he must be playing a very clever waiting game – mind you, he is Italian and they are supposed to be good at all that kind of thing, aren't they?

Bossy Bowyer and I went through all the regions for the

conferences, they're going to be at all the major venues in Glasgow, Liverpool, Cardiff, Birmingham and London. Bossy Bowyer said that it might be the case that 'Mr Canfield' (a.k.a. ANA) will be coming with me ... 'as your right hand, you understand, Jacqueline.' Does Bossy Bowyer know I fancy ANA? Is that what he was hinting at? Does he feel sorry for me and thinks I won't have a chance with Andy unless we're stuck in some cheesy hotel in Cardiff together? Or maybe he thinks I can't do the job alone but doesn't know how to say that? ... now stop this right now, come on, Jacqueline M Pane, you should be pleased that Andy is going to be with you and leave it at that. STOP trying to find subterfuge when it's not there ... thing is you never know ... STOP IT ... OK, OK ... I've stopped ... (for now).

26 January

As usual, lunch with Sally and of course the inevitable came up again – breast enlargement. Well, in my case reshaping rather than enlargement. It's different for Sally, she's so completely perfect in every way (I suppose she does have that slightly-thick-ankles issue but they're so easy to hide). Naturally, Sally did her usual best friend thing of saying I didn't need to have my breasts reshaped and how lucky I was to have big breasts and how she yearned to have tits that men would look at, blah, blah, blah. Course I told her that big breasts à la Pamela Anderson are one thing but ones that are more like old socks with tangerines dropped in the bottom are an entirely different kettle du poisson. Sally and I then started talking about how, when it actually came down to it, women should only really be interested in men who loved us for ourselves and not for how we looked . . . try as we might, and we do try, I still can't get that to ring completely true. Anyway, Sally was only joining in to make me feel better (as per) because, of course, Lovely Dan does love her exactly the way she is, but then again he hasn't exactly got his work cut out for him because Sally *is* gorgeous . . . apart from the thick ankles and he might not have seen them yet. So all that feminist stuff sounds great but it doesn't feel completely convincing – maybe it will when I've lost half a stone. Told Sally all about ANA and him coming to the conferences and stuff. Oh yeah, Sally had a completely barmy theory . . . she reckoned Andy was behaving funnily at the meeting with Pozzi because he was jealous of the attention Carlo was paying me. Poor Sally, sometimes she just doesn't get it . . . I suppose she's only doing what a best friend does really.

Didn't dare tell Sally I was thinking of liposuction – I just know she'd have a fit. Sometimes I wish I could share my cellulite with someone. I don't mean actually share the cellulite – although that'd be great – I mean share the tyranny of the cellulite. You see, Sally's only got a tiny bit up around where her thighs meet her bum and, get this, she thinks that's normal for a woman over 30! I've got it right down to my feet and I'm sure it's spreading round to the front . . . I wonder if it's like mould – the more there is the more it grows. It's really peculiar the way Sally seems to be able to just accept bits of herself like that, except for her small breasts. I keep telling her that after you've been to bed with someone the first few times they don't seem to stay that interested in your breasts. Especially if, like mine, the total mass forms a reasonably attractive package when contained by a bra – but are a bit like five-day-old party balloons once released. Far from big tits being an advantage for sex, actually you become fixated on not having it in any positions where they are going to look horrible ... and that isn't always that easy ... especially if you want to look like a swinger and not all uptight and old-fashioned.

NB: Include chapter on 'Most Flattering Positions to Have Sex In' when I write my self-help book.

NB: Book that 'Learning to Live without Cellulite' away-day.

Stayed in Saturday night – decided not to go to that party down the road. I was feeling tired and anyway I noticed I'd got a bit of a moustache growing – my period must be on its way. Great little reminder that, now I've turned into a Mexican revolutionary, before I've even got to the stage where I burst into floods of tears because they've run out of pickled gherkins at Sainsbury's.

27 January

Woke up nice and early to ensure there was time for a proper re-examination of recent beard growth in the full light of day. Mercifully, it's still only at the moustache stage and hasn't spread to my chin yet ... maybe, this time, I'll manage to bypass the orthodox rabbi look. Also, it's not quite as dark and hairy as it seemed last night but decided to 'Jolen Cream Facial Bleach' it anyway, just to be on the safe side. God, that stuff burns ... I read the ingredients and I'm sure it's got some of the same stuff in it that eliminates limescale ... I suppose that doesn't matter too much as long as it also eliminates the Charles Bronson effect.

Decided to go to the gym and do an exercise class with

Gillian the Nazi. I tried to stay at the back as usual but there weren't very many people there this morning and Mein Führer made me stand at the front so that the new people could follow me. Honestly, I wanted to die – three years of decoy technique, executed with military precision, completely down the pan. I'd deliberately changed classes erratically, missing one here, turning up at three in a row there, etc. so that no one single teacher would think I was a regular and then submit me to the Gestapo-like torture of getting me to show an exercise to newcomers. Gillian didn't actually get me to do anything on my own but, standing at the front, all I could feel, as we pounded the floor with those bloody star-jumps, was every pair of eyes behind me transfixed by that shelf of solid fat that has made its permanent resting place in the previously unclaimed, unnamed territory above my buttocks and below my waist. I didn't even know that bit of my body existed until that shelf appeared there. Terrific, isn't it? The older you get the more new places restless fat finds to make its home. I was waving down a taxi the other day (NB: never do that again in a sleeveless dress) and discovered that the flesh on my upper arm was still shuddering to a standstill *after* I'd got into the cab. It's bad enough that new nooks and crannies are being sought out on a daily basis by fugitive fat but now it appears that this new kind of fat moves at a different rhythm to the rest of my body! My buttocks definitely have a mind of their own and that shelf is completely independently spirited. I never thought I'd be looking back longingly at my 20s, it's not as if I was thin then but at least the fat all seemed to move as one. Nowadays, there's no telling which spare tyre is going to bring attention to itself when you least expect it. I saw some bodysuit thing in an American mail order catalogue – it was like a girdle only it didn't just keep your stomach flat like a 'panty-girdle' (NB: never use the word panty, even if you go to

America). Anyway, from the bottom up, it started like shorts, sort of thing, except from below your knees, then went all the way up to your neck and down your arms to the bend in your elbows. It looked really useful, because at least that way you could squash and unify the movement of your excess weight, but the only thing was I couldn't work out what you could wear it with – course that's assuming you could move at all, once you had it on. A polo neck and trousers might be alright with that underneath but if you wanted to go out you'd have to be carried to your destination on a stretcher because I really don't think bending in it is a possibility. It looked a bit like a wet suit. Goodness, it's bad enough wearing control pants – I wore a pair once, when in a fit of madness I'd bought a very clingy dress. Thing is, they were so effective in their 'control' that they were more like a tourniquet than a pair of pants and they cut off the blood supply to my feet. I had a bit of trouble walking for a couple of days after that but it was worth it because loads of people had said how slim I looked in that dress. God, those were the days . . . I wonder if I've still got those control pants . . . I could wear them under my swimming costume when I go on holiday.

   NB: Period started in the night – I feel all bloated and leaden. No change there, then.

30 January

Didn't have much to write yesterday. Sorry. Stayed in most of the day trying to decide whether or not to take radical action with the moustache and resort to a razor (not to kill myself, to shave with) – decided that shaving would probably be a bit of a mistake at this stage, it might have all sorts of unwelcome repercussions – like a full beard by the end of the year.

Popped in to see Old Mrs Mellish across the hall, see if she was alright or needed anything. I had to get out of the flat anyway because the new bloke in the flat downstairs turns out to have an active and loud sex life. Bloody hell, I thought they were using a megaphone. Just my luck, not only is he rampant but noisy with it.

NB: Do not raise eyebrows in knowing fashion when I pass him on the stairs.

31 January

Started the planning for the Pozzi conferences in earnest today. ANA and I were discussing dates to visit the venues and suddenly he said, 'So shall we have that drink tomorrow, then?' – I didn't know what to say! I mean, I wanted to just say, 'Yes, that'd be lovely' obviously, but I couldn't, could I? Then he might have thought I'd been waiting all this time for him to ask, I mean I know I have but I don't want *him* to know that. He'd go off me if he thought I liked him. If he knew I actually *wanted* to have a drink with him. Everybody immediately goes off people who like them back, don't they? ... Mmm, maybe normal people like people who like them, just like that – God, wouldn't life be simple if that's how it really was? Anyway, I couldn't believe it, these words came out of my mouth ... 'I can't manage tomorrow, maybe some other time'!!!!! It was like in *The Exorcist*, when that little girl's head spins round and she says something about her mother knitting socks in hell or something. This voice just came out of my mouth – all cool and unavailable ... ME! He looked a bit downcast and I felt really sorry for him but at least he doesn't think I like him and had been waiting to be asked. I do feel a bit stupid, though, but I suppose that's better than having a sleepless night worrying about what I'd order in the pub that would make me look interesting. God, what if he never asks again, what if that was my one and only chance? What if he only liked me enough to ask once? Oh, my God ... what have I done? It's not as if I even wanted to say what I said, it just plopped out of my mouth because I was panicking that he felt he *had* to ask me for a drink, you know, because he'd already mentioned it and now we were working together and he didn't want to appear like he'd forgotten or was being rude or anything. Perhaps I can make it up tomorrow when I go in. I could just offer to go to bed with him without bothering about the drink to make up for the insult. Steady on, Jackie, that's not very sensible, is it – he may not regard sex with me as a big treat, probably more of a consolation prize ... no, I'll have to think of something else.

NB: Take different route home when pondering issues of importance, such as PNBs (Potential New Boyfriends), do not take short cut via McDonald's – the answer to your problems does not lie in a party size box of Chicken McNuggets.

1 February

Managed to avoid ANA at work most of the day, bit of a strain as we were supposed to carry on planning the Pozzi conferences but every time he came into the office I pretended to be talking on the phone. I made it sound as if half the calls were sort of businessy and professional, lots of 'Mmm, yes . . . I can see how that would be an advantage, given your budget' . . . and a few 'Well, I'm quite tied up at the moment . . . mmm . . . yes . . . I'll see if there's someone else in the office that could help.' All that was quite easy but by the fourth time he'd come in I realised I'd better look as if my normal working day was also peppered with some sort of interesting social life, so I did a bit of laughing during one pretend call, followed by some 'Well, that would be great but not for a couple of weeks because I'm pretty busy at the moment', then I panicked and realised Andy might think that the 'busyness' came from having a boyfriend or something, so on the next call I made it look as if I was comforting a friend, lots of 'Yes, I see,' and 'Oh, poor you'. ANA looked a bit puzzled by the fifth time he'd seen me on the phone. I hope he doesn't check with the switchboard operator and find out that I never actually dialled out and no one called in. God, it was hard work, I don't think I'm very good at improvising.

I'm beginning to think it might just be easier to have a drink with him.

4 February

You will never believe it! Andy asked me out again today! NB: Must have worked, all the fake phone calls/interesting life stuff. This time I decided not to risk it and just said yes. So, after work we went for a drink in the pub and guess what – it was really nice, we just chatted and it was all quite easy.

That was probably because I'd worked out my regime for the drink thing in advance. He thought I was having spritzers all evening but when he went to the bar I always made sure he got the wine in one glass and the fizzy water in another – I said I preferred mixing it myself. Then when he wasn't looking I chucked the wine into a nearby ornamental plant and put the water into the wine glass. That way I didn't look like some sanctimonious teetotaller making him feel like he was an alcoholic or something but I was able to keep perfect track of everything that was happening because I had a completely clear head. I really admire Andy for asking me out again, I wouldn't have. Anyway, we had a nice time, I think . . . well, I did, God, I hope he did, he didn't seem to want to leave but maybe he was being polite . . . no, I think he wanted to stay talking to me because he was asking loads of questions about my life. He seemed really interested in me . . . weird, huh? It felt very strange someone wanting to know stuff about me . . . I wonder what that's about. Came home feeling quite cheerful and chuffed . . . WOW, what if he likes me as I am? No, that isn't very likely, he probably hasn't realised what I look like in the nude . . . God, I can't even bear to think about it.

NB: Do not get ahead of yourself, there is no nudity on the horizon, cross that bridge when you come to it, or rather don't cross that bridge if you can help it, stay fully clothed for as long as poss.

We had loads to talk about apart from work and when we were saying goodbye at the bus stop (he bicycles to work) I felt really lazy saying I didn't sprint home or something. Anyway, he said, 'Maybe we could have dinner next time.' Gosh, he must like me a bit if he wants to have dinner. Unless it's a test to see how much I eat. Now that he knows I don't use the journey to work as an exercise opportunity maybe he wants to see how much of a sloth I really am.

NB: Take that see-through bag with gym things to work tomorrow, leave on top of desk all day.

6 February

I was getting on with the schedule for the Pozzi conferences on the master plan board that's up on the wall when Andy walked into the room. When I heard him come in, I managed to whip round and keep my bum against the wall for the whole time he was in the room. Gosh, that was a close one, he nearly walked in and got a full-on view of my bottom – which he was bound to compare to the massive chart covering the entire back wall. Anyway, he obviously didn't see it, in its hideous entirety, because he asked me to have dinner with him on the 14th. He said he was sorry it wasn't sooner but that he wanted to go to a particular restaurant on that day.

God, I'm so nervous, I'll bet he doesn't realise that the 14th is Valentine's Day. The whole restaurant will be filled with couples in love not panicking about their fat knees throughout their meals. The waiters are going to notice that we aren't in love and will probably think Andy is my brother who has taken me (his old spinster sister, who doesn't get out much) for a meal on Valentine's Day just to be nice to her. I'm not sure I can bear the pressure of our first date being on Valentine's Day – oh, get a load of that, 'our first date', for all I know he's bringing a friend and it's not a date date at all. It must be a mistake him making the date for Valentine's Day – he can't be that romantic and nice and normal – he wouldn't fancy me if he were all those things.

8 February

I was just beginning to feel fab what with THE dinner to look forward to and everything ... well, I say look forward to, I mean I am sort of looking forward to it but I realise for the date to go really well I'll have to have lost some weight beforehand, so I am now starving myself. I've worked it out, there are six days left until the dinner. If I eat nothing at all in that time I could lose ... say eight pounds, a pound and a half a day, that's feasible, isn't it? Especially if I don't drink anything – even water. Thing is I do have to work during the next few days and it's quite hard what with those annoying mini-blackouts I get when I don't eat. I suppose I could just have a little water to keep me going and maybe the odd glucose tablet.

Anyway, things were going fine and then *they* came back, my dad and stepmother Jennifer. I'd completely forgotten they were coming back so soon, I thought they were away for at least another month, rushing round the globe ruining other people's lives. I got home and there was a message from Jennifer on the answermachine ... 'Hello, there (what sort of greeting is hello there, what is she, a ranch-hand?), Jack (if I've told her once not to call me Jack, I've told her one million times, I know she does it to let me know that she thinks of me as a silly, insignificant, androgynous, Jack type of person), it's Jennifer and Daddy here, we're back from our travels and longing to see you, hope all's well, do give us a ring when you can, bye now.'

My father's wife Jennifer is ghastly, interfering, undermining, meddling, and worst of all ... gorgeous, absolutely drop-dead gorgeous and very bright and nice. She has two grown-up children (from her previous marriage), Beatrice known as Bee (yuk) and Kyle (oh, pleeeeeze). Naturally they are both effortlessly thin and successful – mmm, sort of goes without saying, doesn't it? Dad probably only picked Jennifer once he'd found out she had children younger than me who could serve as a constant reminder to me that I am not perfect in every (or any) way. Now that Dad's retired they've been travelling around trying to find somewhere abroad to live, it's either going to be Italy or Portugal. They've saved enough money to get a house with a pool – can't wait to go for a visit, mmm, hopefully coinciding with Bee and Kyle. Oh, there's nothing that thrills me more than the prospect of appearing in my bikini in front of those two and Jennifer, oh and my Dad, complete with raised eyebrow and all. It's funny the way a parent's raised eyebrow can do more damage to your psyche than, say, Chinese water torture. Maybe it's just the way my dad raises his eyebrows – he's got a lovely, special judgmental way of doing it. Sally says her mum does it too, she reckons all parents attend seminars called 'How to Ruin Your Child's Life with Facial Expressions'. My mum obviously went to the same place but specialised in 'Wrecking Children's Lives with Your Lips'. Her preferred method is a pinched mouth technique, sort of 'I'm not going to say anything, but if you had any idea of the mistake you are making' kind of puckered lips that look like a hen's arse. Can't think why Mum and Dad didn't stay together. When they went out for a meal, between them they could reduce the most robust waiter to a snivelling mass, never mind the fun they could have had together wrecking the rest of my life. Between Mum's hen's arse mouth and Dad's aerobic eyebrows, it's a wonder I've ever made a decision about anything.

Oh, I must stop this, and focus exclusively on getting skeletal for the 14th and then everything will be brilliant. Andy will adore me, particularly if I don't eat that night either. Maybe I should jog to the restaurant so that I look really fit and healthy. I'm not sure I'll be able to manage that – I passed out when I ran for the bus the other day and the stop's only 100 yards from my front door. It was really embarrassing – when I came to, there was a whole load of people crowded round, staring down at me, as I lay in an unseemly heap on the pavement. I knew they were all thinking, 'People like her shouldn't be running for buses, they should be getting boy scouts to wheel them across the road and do their shopping and stuff.' Anyway, at least I got my bus.

I wish Dad and Jennifer hadn't come back before my date with Andy, now I'll feel even more like a failure if Andy doesn't raise the topic of our future children's education during the first course. 'Our children', I'm completely running amok, I must stop this, I must stop this planning ahead thing before I've got to know someone. Sally's boyfriend Dan says I give off the wrong messages to blokes, he says when men first meet women they want to be getting the sort of signals that say, 'I can't wait to be naked with you.' He says that I look like I'm thinking, 'Do you fancy a stroll past the local Mothercare?' He also said I hadn't got 'bedroom eyes', I'd got 'pram eyes'. It's not as if I think about getting married and having kids all the time but it is true that the moment I'm interested in someone I start doodling dresses with trains in tulle and taffeta and I don't even know what tulle is.

I've obviously got some sort of Pavlov reflex to men. Pavlov reflex is that thing when you show a dog a piece of meat and ring a bell at the same time – after you've done it enough times, you only have to ring the bell and the dog will salivate, even without seeing the meat. If a bloke asks me the time of day often enough, after a while I only have to look at my watch to imagine myself saying 'I do' and driving a Volvo estate filled with children dressed in Baby Gap clothes. God, the clothes are sweet in that shop, they are so adorable I just have to look at them and I'm ready to jump on the first passer-by and beg him to impregnate me.

Can't sleep. That Downstairs Man is at it again – don't know if it's the same girl, this one is making very peculiar noises, it sounds like she's coxing for the Oxford boat-racing team. Probably what every man dreams of – a loudly appreciative shag, not like me, I'm sure I'm less of a bang and much more of a whimper.

9 February

Bought a new dress for the dinner with Andy today. I got one a size too small – sort of as an added incentive to keep going with this fasting thing. I can just about get into it now, it's a longish dress with buttons all the way down the front. I've got to admit that where the buttons do up around my tits, they are sort of straining at the leash, kind of hanging on for dear life, but they should be alright by the time of the dinner. They'd better be, otherwise when I sit down, a position, I've checked, which puts even more strain on the buttons, one of them might not be able to take the pressure for a moment longer and will fly off and take Andy's eye out. Great, then I'll be responsible for blinding him. Mind you, if Andy was blind he wouldn't be able to see what I look like in the nude and that wouldn't be such a bad idea. Bet I'd be the only person in the world a disabled person would feel sorry for.

Anyway, the shop assistant kept trying to hint that I should try the next size up but I was able to withstand her withering cruelty because I just *knew* I would soon be thinner and would probably find that size far too big. When she was busy doing something else and not looking at me, I did actually try on the next size up and it did look much better but I couldn't let her win like that, so I had to buy the smaller one – hope I don't regret it. I can't even exchange it now in case that same assistant is in there, she'll know she was right and revile me for deluding myself that I was capable of being thinner than I am and then I'll never be able to go into that shop again and then . . . oh, I could always get Sally to exchange it I suppose.

10 February

Did three really gruelling classes in a row this morning at the gym – gosh, exercising is hard when you haven't eaten for a while. Felt a bit wobbly on my legs and a bit peculiar – I think I've gone into that trippy state of mind Picasso and all his mates did when they were starving in attics in Paris or something. I remember, when I was at school, going to some art gallery and seeing some weird paintings of cardboard boxes walking downstairs and bits of bicycles floating in the air. The art teacher explained that they'd all been done when the artists, who were too poor to eat, had started hallucinating through hunger. Hope I don't start doing that at work, don't think Bossy Bowyer would take too liberal a view of me rambling on about bike spokes in the clouds in the middle of a sales pitch.

I've been thinking maybe I should have therapy. Sally thinks I should. She said, 'Anybody who thinks the success of a date depends on the visibility of her ribcage definitely needs therapy.' She was very cross when I wouldn't eat anything at lunch the other day. She went on and on about Andy liking me for who I was and saying that as he'd already asked me out I didn't need to be thinner for the date and all that stuff and also that if he *did* prefer me thinner then what did it say about him. I know she's right (sort of) in one way and I know it makes sense and everything but I don't really feel hunger any more ... more evangelical than hungry, like I've gone to a higher plane kind of thing ... maybe Joan of Arc was just dieting and not a visionary. Anyway, I will consider therapy, I've bought this book, *The Twisted Path to Therapy* by Jurgen Kraus, Dip. Psycho. Pathos, MD, here's an interesting bit I've photocopied ...

'Therapy varies in disciplines. Essentially therapy aims to aid the patient to accept themselves as they are, rather than spending their lives fantasising that there is a 'perfect place' to be, a 'perfect self' to attain. Therapy can offer many changes but the greatest and most all-encompassing is acceptance, acceptance of oneself and one's circumstances, helping a patient make the most of their opportunities. A patient should expect naturally to endeavour to 'engage' the therapist at first, such as looking for affirmation, approval, commonly known as 'feedback'. This is a normal process during the initial stages of the therapeutic dynamic wherein the patient is the child and they are trying to be loved, ipso facto approved of, by the parent/therapist. This is the first stage of the relationship which develops, soon enough.'

Well, that sounds quite good (clearly not written to cater for someone who is starting therapy whilst overweight, though). I guess they are assuming that you'd have lost weight before you actually started. There's no mention of 'accepting' yourself as fat – obviously, I suppose. So maybe I will give it a try when I've lost a few more pounds. That last bit puzzled me a bit, though. I'm no more likely to be asking a stranger to approve of me than I am to pour molten lava into my ears. If I had the confidence to seek approval from a stranger, and what's more a paid stranger, I'd hardly be likely to be in therapy, would I??!!

It says that there are various ways to find a therapist but the most normal route (odd choice of words that, normal, in the circumstances) is through your GP. Not entirely happy about going through my doctor because Dad and Jennifer use the same surgery, when they're here, and what if the doctor mentioned it to Jennifer. I know about ethics and everything but she may think it's relevant for my father's wife to know or even that it's just too juicy a piece of gossip not to pass on. I suppose I could ask the doctor at work ... oh, yeah, right, that's a good idea, alternatively I could hire a Zeppelin to fly over the Greater London area for a day with JACQUELINE IS A LOSER – SHE IS HAVING THERAPY written on the side. I don't think the doctor at work is deliberately indiscreet but, on reflection, he may have realised that the bulletin board was not the best place to inform the boys in the production department who'd gone on that Amsterdam weekend what their test results were.

No, I'll just write to one of the therapy clinics direct, the book says you can do that. Then there'll be no way anybody will find out ... unless the postman recognises the envelope – oh, honestly, how paranoid can you be, Jackie, get a grip on yourself. The postman is hardly likely to know an envelope a psychotherapist uses from one the gas board uses, unless he's a descendant of Freud's and that's not very likely because they are all in the media and don't work for the Post Office, I'm pretty sure.

11 February

Haven't been able to write anything for a couple of days. Sorry. I have been transfixed with a horrible thought – what if Andy either comes back here, to my flat, with me after THE dinner (unlikely, I realise) or wants to pick me up beforehand and Downstairs Man is mid-indulging in audible sex, as per usual? Andy might think I've asked my neighbour to have a hefty shag, so that it puts the idea of loving in his mind. If that *does* happen, I'll just have to put some loud music on. Even better – I could just not let Andy in and just go straight down when he buzzes. That's probably the best idea, because I'm not too sure about him seeing my flat anyway. I did think that pale pink in the living room was kind of cool and breezy but he might think it looks like Barbie's ice-cream parlour and Sally's Dan says the bathroom looks like a brothel for poodles, maybe lime green and black wasn't so fab after all. Perhaps I should repaint the whole flat before THE dinner with Andy – is that a bit keen? . . . and anyway I don't know what colours he likes – suppose I could have a quick look round his desk when he's out . . .

13 February

Been so fixated with THE dinner overshadowing my life like a spectre that I've hardly been able to concentrate at work. Having a few problems working out the timing for the conferences, some of the venues have clashes so we may have to change the schedule a bit. It was originally supposed to be Cardiff – end of March, Liverpool – mid-April, Birmingham

– beginning of May, Glasgow – early June and ending up with London – mid-July. It's Cardiff and Glasgow that are causing difficulties, so I suppose I can juggle them without too much upheaval. It's my brief anyway so nobody need know that it differs from the original plan.

NB: Take home and destroy all previous paperwork concerning original plan. Thin Clare may see it and use it as ammunition against me in the future.

I'm going to have to face a weekend at Mum's after the Birmingham conference. Her house is only about 40 minutes from the centre, so I guess there's no way out of that one.

Dad called me at work today, did a nice line in 'why didn't you call us back' guilt. As if I didn't have enough to feel panicked about, what with THE dinner looming, THE dinner at which my entire future will be decided! Told Dad I'd been really busy etc. I could hear Jennifer in the background saying, 'What's her news?' Honestly, that woman missed her vocation – she'd have made a super traffic warden. How can a person make one word sound so evil – 'news', 'news', 'news', indeed. I know very well what she means by that. Of course, what she really means is 'Has she got engaged, if not, has she at least got a boyfriend even, or has she been promoted at work ... in short, has she done *anything* of note while we've been away?' In a mad fit of panic I went and said, 'Yeah, actually, I've got a new boyfriend but it's early days and there's nothing much to report yet.' OH MY GOD – what on earth possessed me to say that! I've really done it now ... why didn't I just bike my diary over to Jennifer with a note saying, 'Feel free to dip into this and read at your leisure. PS: Don't miss the bits about you and your kids.' It would have been quicker and a lot less painful. It just popped out, I couldn't help myself, the prospect of not having anything interesting to say turned me into a throbbing mass of competitive jealousy. Oh, I guess

I should calm down, it's probably a bit much to have reacted so badly to the word 'news', isn't it?

NB: To be on the safe side, create interesting new boyfriend profile to have readily to hand should Jennifer ask questions about him next time I see her – get background details fully memorised. If I get caught off guard I may say something ludicrous, like he's a film star or a major politician. Actually that's not a bad idea because then I'd have to be secretive about him, wouldn't I?

Anyway, I think I've got the Pozzi conferences schedule under control. Better had soon, that Carlo Pozzi rang again today! Not quite sure if he's got anything else to do. He never asks what the developments are with the conferences, he just rings up and chats and asks how I am and how things are going and stuff like that. What on earth is he playing at? Mmm, maybe he's doing my trick of pretending he's got an interesting life to someone in his office too.

4 a.m. Can't sleep – it's partly the starvation thing which is making me feel a bit floaty but mainly I am being kept awake by trying to work out a load of witty and amusing things to say tomorrow night at THE dinner ... oh, no, it's tonight now, isn't it? The only trouble with trying to work out your conversation in advance is that you don't know what the other person is going to say. If I can't know exactly what Andy's going to say (which would be difficult, I know) then it'd be great if I knew what sort of things, at least, he was going to talk about. Then I could prepare some stories around those subjects that would make me look appealing and intelligent. I'll make a list of likely topics and some good responses, then I'll ring Sally and go over them with her.

NB: Don't phone Sally till around 7 a.m. – Dan gets annoyed if I wake them up too early, particularly since he thinks it's bonkers.

MY DINNER WITH ANDY
POSSIBLE SUBJECTS – GOOD RESPONSES

If he asks about work – say everything's under control and tell a light-hearted story about Mr Bowyer and car parking space incident – it doesn't matter that there isn't one, make something up. Caution – do not imply that men are sometimes silly about their cars – especially expensive ones.

If he asks anything about where I live – do not mention Downstairs Man and frequency of sexual intercourse, do mention Old Mrs Mellish, her seniority of age and that I go in to see her regularly. Caution – if brought up, ensure that visits to Mrs M. sound as if they are fitted in, with some considerable difficulty, around action-packed social life, not other way round.

If he asks about my family – do not mention that mother can reduce me to tears with hen's arse mouth. Do not say father is married to paragon of virtue. Do not mention stepsister Bee, he might like the sound of her. Say that we are a close-knit family and see each other regularly. This is necessary for two reasons – one, it's much less interesting to talk about than bitter and twisted Mum in Worcestershire and undermining Dad and wife – two, I might look a little neurotic if I tell him about my family.

If he asks about previous relationships – do not mention Perfect Peter or that he took a job in New York, I will look like someone who is so clingy that people have to cross large oceans to shake me off. Only say that there has been 'no one special for a while', and then I don't look either like a nun or a prostitute – just something in between and that's about right – that's the sort of thing men want, isn't it?

I think that's just about covered everything, hasn't it? I mean if he talks about arts or films or books (oh, help) or anything that I haven't prepared an answer for, I'll just have to rely on my natural wit and brilliant mind – hah! Looks like he'll be doing most of the talking, then.

14 February

6 a.m. – HELP ME, GOD – LET ME DIE NOW, I CAN'T BEAR THE ANTICIPATION A MOMENT LONGER.

9 a.m. – panic stations, fell asleep after writing the above and overslept, running late, no time to double-check possible topics with Sally (I'll fax her the list at her office. NB: Use code, in case someone at her office knows Andy).

Got to work on time. Confession. Look, I'd better get it out in the open, I ate about four, well, four and a half of those almond croissants on my way to work. I was starving and I hadn't slept most of the night and I thought I might pass out and go into a hypoglycaemic coma and end up missing THE dinner completely . . . and anyway, the buttons on that dress are now doing up comfortably . . . well, if I sit up straight. Anyway, I've got so much adrenalin coursing through my body, the calories from the croissants couldn't possibly get to my breasts before tonight . . . could they?

15 February

Well, I blew it, didn't I? Of course I did, what else would you expect? I blew it, blew it, blew it. I've gone and wrecked my one and only chance of happiness, fulfilment, inner peace, a brood of beautiful children, being Chair of the Neighbourhood Watch, parental respect, promotion, and a small bum – in short, everything. Here goes – might as well commit my shame to the page and posterity . . . perhaps I'll learn something from it – HAH!

Andy came up to me at work and said, 'I'll pick you up at about 7.45 p.m., if that's OK with you.' I said, 'OK, but just press my buzzer and I'll come straight down, they're doing extensive dry-rot repairs in the stairwell and it's all in a mess.' They're not, of course, but I knew I was going to have more than enough on my panicking plate just getting dressed, I couldn't face the added worry of what Andy might conclude if he saw the flashing neon Jesus in the toilet. Hope God doesn't pay me back for lying and give me real dry rot.

Spent the rest of the day at the office rushing up and down the corridor, barking instructions to Thin Clare and New Secretary Sarah, they've probably decided I'm a Rottweiler in a skirt but I just could not stay still.

Oh, yeah, there was a card on my desk when I got in this morning. It was a picture of a big red heart with an arrow through it and it said, 'Looking forward to spending time with you, xxx' – who on earth could have left that and why? Mr Bowyer? Jack, the night cleaner? The bloke in Swansea who's trying to persuade me to add his conference venue to my list of regular venues? Is it *supposed* to be romantic? Is it a Valentine's card? Is there a hidden message in it and I don't get it? This is maddening – I think it should be compulsory to sign Valentine cards, that way everyone knows where they stand and I wouldn't be forced to waste my lunch-hour furtively rooting around my colleagues' desks looking for matching handwriting.

Finished work and raced home, missed the first bus. Well, I

didn't actually miss it as such, I saw, I touched it, but I couldn't get on it. The driver was doing that thing of deliberately closing the doors as I was running towards him. I got so close that the doors almost took my nipples off and then the driver did that 'pretending he couldn't see me', even though I was practically Morris dancing to get his attention, begging him to let me in. Very dignified. Obviously I can't take that bus route again. Plaintive message from Mum on the answerphone and one from Sally wishing me good luck for tonight – I'd completely forgotten to fax her that sheet, hope that wasn't the deciding factor.

Had a bath and managed to take the first three layers of skin off my knee while I was shaving my legs – honestly, you'd think there was a major artery in there – blood everywhere, didn't have time to clean it up.

NB: Now Andy *definitely* couldn't come into the flat, he'd have thought I'd been sacrificing sheep or something.

Of course, didn't have any bandages, so I improvised with a Panty Pad and some gaffer tape, it was quite a deep cut, I had to just pray it wouldn't go gangrenous during dinner. Gosh, wouldn't Andy have fancied me then? – we stand up at the end of a beautiful evening and half my leg falls off under the table.

Squeezed into my new dress, the buttons looked reasonably secure, especially with my minimiser bra. I hadn't had occasion to wear that bra for a while – it does reduce the bulk out front, but obviously the flesh has got to go somewhere, so it sort of spreads it horizontally around you like an inner tube – it felt a bit like I'd got a couple of squishy cucumbers trapped under my armpits.

Andy came to pick me up in a cab and we went to this really nice, very posh-looking restaurant in town. I was very edgy and nervous and instead of dealing with this in a mature, in control, business woman of the '90s way, I plumped for the truculent teenager's option and quelled my nerves with three vodka and tonics on the trot before we'd even been shown to our table. We did talk and stuff, Andy ordered some nice wine and I don't think I was slurring my words all the time. It's hard to remember exactly what happened during the actual meal because I was so pissed once I'd had some wine that it took all the powers I could muster not to lay my head down on the table and have a little nap before the starter arrived.

Anyway, to cut a long story short I have absolutely no idea how the rest of the evening went – what happened after the main course is a complete mystery to me. All I know is that I woke up this morning in my bed, with a mouth that felt like somebody had been baling hay in it, and nothing on except for my minimiser and pants . . . even the makeshift tourniquet had gone, which means that whoever put the dead-weight rag doll that I must have been to bed also dealt with a blood-soaked Panty Pad. I don't know how I got there, I don't what I did and, worst of all, I don't know who undressed me. Now I've got two buttock-clenchingly embarrassing alternatives – either Downstairs Man found me propped up against the main entrance door and took pity on me or Andy brought me home, undressed me and left – in which case, I may as well take a lethal overdose right now. Today's Saturday, so I've got two days to either kill myself or work out what happened before I see him in the office.

NB: If it was Andy, why didn't he take all my clothes off, or was the sight of me, semi-naked, complete with minimiser, so revolting that he bolted as soon as he clapped eyes on it?

Stayed in bed most of the day, couldn't even answer the phone, I just didn't feel strong enough to face anybody, not even Sally – she must have rung about 94 times. Later on, I decided I'd better find out what happened in those lost hours, so I went downstairs to ask Downstairs Man if he had any aspirin. It took all the courage I had to go through with it. Just as I was hovering at his door, he burst out. 'Haven't seen you for ages, how are you?' was the first thing he said, so I made my excuses and slipped upstairs again. Right, well, then, might as well just jump straight out of the window ... clearly even the sight of me in next to nothing and paralytic couldn't tempt Andy, so what chance have I got fully clothed and on best behaviour?? Finally rang Sally back, told her the whole miserable episode, she reckoned that Andy must be a really nice bloke to take care of me like that and not try and take advantage, but, she said, we also had to take into consideration the male point of view, as put forward by Dan, which is that Andy must be gay. Well, obviously that would be a tremendous relief but unlikely I think – unless it was a conversion made that night, the sight of my body having turned him off women for ever. As for the 'really nice bloke' theory, this is where Sally's naïveté lets her down – she is missing one major point – if he were a really nice bloke he wouldn't have asked me out in the first place, would he? Honestly, Sally just doesn't get it sometimes.

I can't see a way out of this. If I commit suicide, my mother will be furious and make me feel really guilty. As for asking Andy what happened, I'd rather have my tongue pierced without an anaesthetic than do that. I don't suppose resigning is really an option ... I suppose I could ask for a transfer but that would take time. Technically speaking I'm senior to Andy at work so I think I'll have to opt for freezing him out if he approaches me (which, of course, he'll probably never do again) and not using the lift nearest his office. The latter may be the most radical as I've still got to pass his office to get to the other lifts which is going to make me look a bit silly but is vital under these circumstances.

16 February

I had my work cut out for me trying to get the caked-on blood off the tiles in the bathroom today. What with the ignominy provided by the rest of that evening, I'd completely forgotten about the self-mutilation shaving episode – I got a real fright when I went in and turned the light on, it looked like they'd been doing a remake of *Psycho* in there. It took me the best part of the day and two bottles of liquid Flash to get it clean. Maybe I should start waxing my legs. The only thing is, you have to wait until you've got a hefty amount of growth before you can use that stuff and I'd probably have to wait for my legs to look like Sean Connery's back, which is very hairy and would not be very attractive on a leg . . . come to that, it's not very attractive on a back either . . . I wonder if I've got any hair on *my* back?

NB: Check with hand-held mirror in bathroom mirror.

Seeing as I was up to full speed on personal shame and degradation, I decided to go the whole hog and return Mum's call. In for a penny, in for a pound. Usual couple of minutes about me not calling her often enough, etc. etc., then she started on about Dad's sixtieth birthday coming up . . . 'Do you know if he's planning anything, not that it's any concern of mine, I would hardly expect to be invited, why should I be, although I don't see why not, I did spend thirty years with your father and . . .' I turned the TV on and started channel-hopping with the sound off once she embarked on her old favourite 'why-I-should-be-included-in-all-events-that-I-have-no-interest-in-attending' routine. Mum must have X-ray ears because suddenly I heard 'You're channel-hopping with the sound off, aren't you? I can hear that clicking' . . . naturally I hotly denied it, throwing the channel changer halfway across the living room to get rid of the evidence, but she knew. For a moment, I toyed with the idea of placating her with a few personal titbits and telling her about Andy but I couldn't face the prospect of one of her seminars on ladylike behaviour. My mother thinks the only way to keep a man is to pretend you have no bodily functions – she's still convinced that Dad asked for a divorce because he once saw her on the toilet. No doubt she'd have some helpful and interesting theories on how to regain the respect of a man who's witnessed you in such a high state of intoxication that you passed out and had to be carried home.

Oh, I can't face tomorrow. I hope Andy doesn't get there first and type up a memo entitled something witty like 'Drinking – the Paneless Way'. God, I hate my last name, I used to get all that 'what a Pane' stuff at school and then at college it was 'Pane-ful' when I went into a class, and when I was leaving, 'Oh, we're Pane-less' – most amusing.

17 February

Got into the office and before I'd had time to think about what Andy was doing by the coffee machine with Thin Clare, an enormous bunch of red roses arrived for me, with a card saying 'These should have come with the card'!! I was so embarrassed – New Secretary Sarah and some of the other girls all stood around my desk oooing and ahhing over the flowers, and I could see Andy and Thin Clare looking over. I'm sure they thought I'd sent them to myself to make me look desirable and sought-after. In that book I've got, *34 Steps to Make That Man Marry You*, it suggests you send yourself a flamboyant bouquet to make your boyfriend (or whoever you're trying to get to marry you) think you've got some secret admirer and get all jealous. It was one of the books I bought when things were going off with Perfect Peter – I hadn't managed to get to the end of it before he left me ... if I'd been a quick reader, who knows what might have happened? Thin Clare's engaged – what if it's because she read that book too (obviously *all* of it) and decides to tell Andy it's a ploy? I know it actually isn't but who's to know that – who's going to believe that the flowers are simply from somebody who likes me? Anyway, they were a sort of blessing in disguise because it meant there was a distraction and I didn't have to deal with the whole Andy issue immediately. Got a lot of stuff organised and in-line for the Pozzi schedule, had a quick meeting with Bossy Bowyer – he seems pleased with the developments – it's amazing how well you work when you're desperate to avoid something else, isn't it?

Just as I was leaving at the end of the day, thanking my lucky stars that I'd avoided Andy, he got into the lift I was in. Of course, I broke into a cold sweat – I was terrified that he was going to bring up THE dinner, right there in a lift filled with people. I had to think quick – so I dropped all my papers on the floor (he probably thinks I've got the DTs). Anyway, everybody helped me get them together and as I stood up sorting my things out I realised that Andy was standing there, holding my handbag – funny that he didn't feel silly doing that. I just said, 'Thanks very much, oh, that's my bus' and ran off. I can't display a new lack of co-ordination in the lift every day, I'll have to think up some suitable excuses before tomorrow.

Popped in to Old Mrs M. when I came in this evening, told her about my night of shame, we had a bit of a giggle about it. She nearly wet herself laughing when I told her the bit about the tourniquet, she said she was tickled pink by the picture of a man flapping around trying to dispose of 'one of those things with a dry-weave top sheet and wings for added protection'. She also said, 'Well, he's seen you at your worst now, it can only get better.' I didn't have the heart to tell her about my extensive cellulite – between that and the alcoholic binge, you're a bit spoilt for choice as to which qualifies for 'me at my worst', and that's completely leaving aside the whole pendulous breasts issue. However, it was nice to see the débâcle from a lighter angle . . . it's a pity the only person I can really be myself with is a seventy-three-year-old, housebound, retired court usher who's losing her hearing.

NB: Check audibility from other locations within house of conversations held in Old Mrs M.'s flat. If hip-to-thigh-zone activities in Downstairs Man's flat are as audible to me, as has proven to be the case, then it's possible he can hear everything said in her flat, particularly bearing in mind the decibel level required to get message through to her.

NB: Felt a bit cheered up, confirmation of my booking for that 'Learning to Live without Cellulite' away-day has arrived. It's a one-day intensive on the third Saturday in March in a disused mosque in Crawley – so that's something to look forward to. I wonder where it's actually held . . . I don't think women can go into mosques, well, not wearing their shoes, anyway.

18 February

Didn't see ANA for the whole day at work. First of all I was really relieved, then I began to panic that he'd got himself transferred or something. Turned out he's gone on a training course and he won't be back till next Monday – I don't suppose there is any chance that he could have forgotten about the incident by then ...

Carlo Pozzi rang, we went through the conference schedule and the confirmed venues, and I told him what the current rough timetable was, I think he was happy with everything so far. As we were ending the call, he suddenly said, 'Did you like your flowers?' Bloody marvellous! Thanks a lot, Thin Clare, blabbing about me to a client ... I suppose it could have been New Secretary Sarah, she might have mentioned it to him ... either way it must have been someone in the office – how else would he know about them? I said that they were lovely and everything, but that I didn't know who they were from, and then he said the oddest thing – 'Don't you realise you've got a secret admirer?' I said, 'No, that's very unlikely, it's probably my best friend Sally trying to make me look popular and attractive,' at which he laughed very loudly and said, 'Well, she wouldn't have to try very hard.' I must say, he is most peculiar ... I don't suppose it's possible that he's in on some practical joke the whole office has cooked up? I should never have said that thing about Sally sending the flowers, it makes me look a bit pathetic, not exactly the behaviour of a hard-nosed professional, is it? I mustn't get all worried about this, he was probably just making conversation and trying to be friendly. He might be one of those people you know professionally, who don't know what to talk about on a personal level, so they ask your receptionist or somebody if anything of note has happened in the office recently. If the lifts had broken down he'd probably have tried to start a conversation about hydraulics.

Spoke to Dad, arranged to go and see them tomorrow evening – oh, joy, oh rapture. Nearly got caught out. Jennifer called out in the background, 'And tell her to bring her new boyfriend, if she likes' – I caught myself in the nick of time just as I was about to say, 'What boyfriend?' – that was a close shave. I made up some excuse about him not being around at the moment.

NB: If I am feeling very combative tomorrow, I will wear outfit in which I look most overweight – that'll really get to Dad.

NB: Just reread the above. Oh dear, I suppose I really do have to see about therapy, I'll write to the clinic tonight.

I wonder how much detail you put in these kinds of letter? Those places probably get inundated with requests, and might operate a kind of 'bonkers pecking order' – the more mad you are the quicker you get seen. Well, as I've taken the plunge, I'm not going to hang about waiting for years while some axeman, who's slept with his mother, jumps the queue, I'll make myself sound pretty neurotic. Here we go, then;

Dear The Inner Child Clinic,

Do you suppose you write 'dear' to a clinic? 'To whom it may concern' looks a bit rude, like I've got a complaint or something. Actually if 'Dear' isn't right, then that's quite good, because it makes me look like I don't know how to write a formal letter – that's sort of mad, isn't it?

Dear The Inner Child Clinic,

I am mad – can you help me?

Dear The Inner Child Clinic,

I can only wear jeans when I see my Dad because I know it annoys him to see how big my bum looks – do you think this is normal?

PS For your information, my father is married to a thin woman.

Dear The Inner Child Clinic,

I am having difficulty facing the fact that a Marks and

Spencer size 12 is not a very comfortable fit – what is the answer?

Dear The Inner Child Clinic,

I believe that cellulite is a disease visited upon the unworthy – is that a balanced view?

Why don't I just put all of the above together in one letter and send it like that? It covers a lot of my problem areas and, what's more, it'll read like non sequiturs – which will definitely add to the likelihood of getting me a priority place.

NB: Post the letter from a postbox out of my area, I don't want to run the risk of local sorting office recognising my writing.

NB: I think my period may be approaching, no notable increase in facial hair but cried when I saw the Queen Mother tottering around some opening on the evening news. I've obviously got to that joyous PMT stage when I cry if I see someone miss a bus but wish I was armed when I get a wonky trolley at Sainsbury's.

NB: Buy new box of Panty Pads (heavy to medium flow).

19 February

Really cracked on at work today, what with Andy being away, it's great not worrying about anybody being around to catch me looking inelegant or anything. Had a bite to eat at lunch-time with Thin Clare, I've decided she's alright actually. She was talking about her boyfriend Paul and she told me that it was him who wanted to get married and that she would prefer to stay living together and leave it at that. I wonder if she was just saying that so I wouldn't feel left out?

She then said that, although she was devoted to Paul, she did often wonder what it was like to be independent, 'and able to go out with anyone you wanted and not tied down, like you, Jacqueline' – oddly enough, I think she really meant it. It makes me wince when I hear Mum refer to me as 'her independent daughter'. (Query: why does the word 'independent' sound more like 'lesbian' or 'on the shelf' or 'no idea of how to hold down a relationship' or 'a complete disappointment to me in every way' when uttered by a mother?) But I actually don't think Thin Clare was trying to insult me . . . funny that. Well, doesn't Paul sound like a strange character? I've never imagined it that way round – a man putting pressure on a woman to get married. I wonder if Paul read that *34 Steps . . .* book? He'd have had to modify some of the advice, though, one bit insists you give your boyfriend blowjobs every night until he pops the question. Mmm, that may have been one of the countless areas where I went wrong with Perfect Peter – keen as I was, I simply could not swallow something on a daily basis that involved the ingestion of more calories than there are in a ham sandwich.

NB: I think sperm classifies as an 'empty calorie', like the ones in booze and fruit juices, where nothing of substance is digested but you still get fat from drinking it.

Just got back from Dad and Jennifer's. Surprisingly he didn't say anything about me looking fatter but he did arch his eyebrows as I took a handful of the Luxury Nut Selection Jennifer had deliberately put out to taunt me while we were having a drink before supper. Paid him back for this degradation by eating a three-pack of Ferrero Rocher on the way home. Otherwise the evening was alright. They told me they'd found somewhere in Portugal, they wanted to know all about what was going on at work and how my flat was and everything. Came home feeling alright until I realised that not one question had been posed about my mythical new boyfriend ... damn, Jennifer was obviously letting me know that she knew I'd been lying from the start ... there'd be no other reason for not asking about him, would there? Mmm, there's always the possibility that they'd taken me at my word when I said there was nothing much to report ... now, which is more likely?

NB: Can't get to sleep, there's not a peep from Downstairs Man's flat. I'd begun to find the creaking springs and his hefty shagging noises positively soporific, sort of like a lullaby. I'd better be careful or the next time I have sex I'll probably fall into a deep sleep the moment the heavy breathing starts – that'd be another Pavlov thing.

21 February

Sorry, haven't had a moment to write at all this week. It's been hectic at work. Guess what? Downstairs Man has invited me to a dinner party in his flat tomorrow night ... I hope it's not because he thinks I never go out and he's doing it out of pity. Oh God, what if it's because he's going away for a year or something and wants me to water his bloody plants and redirect his mail to Guatemala or wherever he's going and move his car if they resurface the road? I suppose that's not hugely likely – he's in plastics, I think, and I don't imagine they visit the jungle for extended periods.

NB: On no account refer to tremendous audibility from my living room of host's sex life during dinner – even if conversation flags dismally. Furthermore, do not refer to host as Downstairs Man ... I think his real name is Richard? er ...

Roger? er ... Charles? No, I think it is Richard ... oh, I'll just wait for someone else to say his name first, his other guests are bound to know it – unless it turns out just to be me and Old Mrs M. – I hope he hasn't invited her. I feel a bit mean saying that, but she's quite capable of humming the theme tune from the Bodyform ad while winking at me – she loves an in joke.

23 February

Sorry, I didn't write yesterday – look, actually, I'm tired of saying I'm sorry ... I don't *have* to write every single day, it's my diary and I can write as often or as little as I want ... alright, I know I *ought* to write every day because it's not really a diary if I don't but it is quite hard, you know, trying to find the time and the inclination every single bloody day. Listen, alright, I am sorry, I will try to write something even if it's only to say hello, or 'slept well last night', or something, OK? Then I suppose I'm sticking to the discipline ... and even one line would count as an entry ... wouldn't it? Oh, I am very ratty, aren't I? I've got very bad PMT, I woke up with an aching jaw, I think I'd been grinding my teeth in the night – I'm surprised I didn't wake up with a mouthful of mercury granules. I've obviously been in heavy denial about Andy, I haven't even thought about him or IT for days – I must be 'blocking it' (as the therapy book says), either that or I just don't care what he thinks about me getting blasted and having to be carried home and that is hardly likely. Sally says it's a healthy sign and that I'm learning to accept myself as I am, warts and all (more like warts, cellulite, moustache, fat bum, weak nails, etc., etc. and all) – AS IF! – dear, oh dear, what is Sally like?

He'll be back at work tomorrow and I guess I'll have to face the music then, assuming he doesn't blank me completely but simply leaves an information leaflet for Alcoholics Anonymous on my desk instead.

Oh, I haven't written about last night at Downstairs Man's (his name *is* Richard, but I don't think that suits him as well as my name for him). There were six of us at dinner – myself (obviously), Downs ... sorry, Richard, a colleague of Richard's called Graham, a couple from Glasgow called May and Will and a depressingly pretty girl called Tory – not, as I thought initially, a name given to her by her parents in a bout of fearsome allegiance to their chosen political party but an infuriatingly cute abbreviation for Victoria – yuk! As the evening progressed I deduced that said Tory makes up the other half of Downstairs Man's audible sex sessions – judging by her foghorn laugh, she's definitely the one that's done some coxing in her time. I had quite a nice evening, except I was the first to be served pudding which I innocently and politely accepted before seeing both May and Tory demur! When will I ever learn? NEVER, EVER get lured into accepting pudding before everyone else at a dinner party – if you do, you are immediately identified as THE FAT, GREEDY ONE and everyone else feels cleansed and full of superiority thereafter by refusing it, it's as if by eating it yourself you make it possible for them not to. They probably all actually want pudding too, but they don't want to eat it now that they've seen THE PORKER wolf it down.

NB: General rule. People only notice you are fat when they see you eat puddings or chocolate. If you must have puddings at a dinner party, then refuse it at the table, but make sure you help clear up, then you're bound to have at least a couple of seconds left alone in the kitchen to cram down all the leftover pudding with no witnesses. IF NO ONE SAW – IT DIDN'T COUNT. It's only when you eat in front of strangers or people that make you feel guilty that food is really fattening.

Actually, now that I think about it, the whole meal seemed to have been planned to make me feel large. I managed to be the last to arrive, despite living upstairs, and Richard cracked some joke about it. The truth is I was ready at six-thirty and the invitation was for eight but I didn't want to be too early and look all uncool and empty-life-ish, so I'd actually been watching telly with the sound off (in case he heard the TV), planning on arriving fashionably late (whatever that is – I wonder if there's a book that tells you exactly how many minutes add up to 'fashionably late', that'd be a good thing to know because I inevitably seem to fall into two undesirable categories, 'Pathetically Early' or 'Too Late to Be Included'). I realise now that to look really cool I should have done a few laps round my flat dropping some heavy objects as I went – when the girls in the ads on telly are late, having their periods, shaving their legs or washing their hair, they're always racing around their houses, hopping on one foot, with their knickers up their cracks, dropping shoes and stuff, aren't they?

That Graham bloke was slightly overweight and I wondered if that's why Richard had invited me – a little fat friend for his little fat friend.

Anyway, it was a nice meal, Richard's a good cook. Will, the Scottish one, was apparently quite an amusing person – I wasn't able to verify this personally as I couldn't understand a word he said but virtually every time he spoke the rest of the guests would burst out laughing or smile at each other. So, unless he had an appalling speech impediment that I also didn't pick up on, I'm assuming he was witty. Eventually, by surreptitiously checking to see when other people looked like they were going to laugh, I worked out my cues for bursting into knowing laughter – once I even managed to look like I'd got the joke ahead of everyone else – I'd spotted his girlfriend breaking into a little smile as he started a story and seized the moment. Of course, being me, I also managed to get it wrong a couple of times, which was more than a little embarrassing – particularly when it turned out that one of Will's stories, the very one I'd elected to meet with wild cackling of the 'oh-here-comes-another-side-splitter!' variety, turned out to be about the wholesale closure of Scotland's dockyards.

I hope I didn't disappoint Downstairs Man by not going home with Chubby Graham. I mean ... he wasn't interested in me, I wasn't interested in him but ... I don't know ... maybe I should have slept with him anyway just to be polite ... I don't like to let my host down.

NB: Unavoidable result of dinner invitation will be a return event at mine – I wonder if I should pay Richard back and invite someone who doesn't speak English at all ... mmm, would that be too childish? Quite aside from anything else, he deserves paying back, because even though we didn't all leave till gone 2 a.m., afterwards the Foghorn could still be heard validating something Richard was doing to her in his bedroom! They probably only did it so I know that they can prepare a delicious and complicated three-course meal, drink masses of wine, clear up and still have the energy for torrid sex ... I probably wasn't up early enough to witness him and Tory charging out of the house for a six-mile run this morning at 7 a.m. – taking the more arduous route past the recycling bin wearing a rucksack filled with the entire evening's empties.

24 February

Finally saw Andy, he came over to my desk to tell me that the Pellet big chiefs wanted him to put together a kind of sales brochure, a sort of 'what the company does and who we are' glossy document to give to clients and send out to prospective clients, like the Labour Party does. He said he needed to sort out times for a photo session for everyone and thought he'd see how I was placed first, as being in control of one of our biggest jobs on at the moment, I was probably snowed under. I was so taken aback that he didn't mention THAT night that I nearly agreed to do the photo session. It goes without saying that under no circumstances will I knowingly allow a photograph to be taken and looked at by other people before I've seen it and, if necessary, had it touched up. I fobbed him off with something about having had professional photographs taken recently for my granny (poor old Granny, I've used her more often as an excuse since she died four years ago than I ever did when she was alive!). I said I'd see if I could find them. Great, so now I'm going to have to spend a couple of hundred quid getting some done on the quiet. Mind you, better to be £200 out of pocket than worrying myself sick about the prospect of Andy and New Secretary Sarah going through the contact sheets sniggering over the ones where I wasn't ready and have got that special look you get when you're being photographed – like you're facing a firing squad or your pants are on the wrong way round.

So, that was that – Andy did not mention THAT night and, in fact, was very pleasant and kind all day. What the hell is going on? Rang Sally to see if she could shed any light on this strange behaviour, she wasn't in and I got Lovely Dan. I told him what had happened and he just said, 'I told you he was gay, he obviously spends so much time dreaming about his butcher or somebody that he's completely forgotten it happened.' After it dawned on me that Dan was winding me up, I pressed him again as to what male game Andy could possibly be playing. 'Has it ever occurred to you, Queline, that he just really likes you and isn't bothered by seeing you legless and doesn't need to make a massive drama, like you have, out of it?' The conversation ended there – well, obviously, Dan wasn't going to stop winding me up so it was useless trying to get him to give me a serious answer.

I was really cross after talking to Dan, so I decided to take my mind off it by going over to see Old Mrs M. Of course, we ended up talking about the whole Andy issue and she agrees with Dan's theory. I don't think she was winding me up, but I do feel like the whole world is against me – why won't they drop this maddening fantasy that Andy really likes me?

25 February

Only saw Andy in passing today. Confirmed all the bookings for the Pozzi venues. Didn't ring Mum to arrange the weekend when we're at the Birmingham one – if I wait long enough she might end up being busy the weekend I suggest. That'll be as good as actually going, won't it? I ring up all keen and willing to spend an entire weekend with her and then it'll turn out she's made other plans – I can then act all sad and disappointed and make *her* feel guilty for a change, and that'll be her sorted until at least Christmas. Nothing much happened at work, apart from there being another delivery of some flowers. My heart dropped as I saw the boy come in with them, I just can't face another bloody scrutinisation from the office, but it turned out they weren't for me – luckily. I got a bit tense and snappy with everyone in the office, it's a combination of the PMT and the 'Andy, sword of Damocles' thing hanging over my head. I cannot believe he's not just casually biding his time waiting to pounce on me with a machinegun-style personality assassination about THAT evening's conduct. It's like waiting to be executed, I wish he'd just drop the guillotine now (as it were) and not prolong the torture longer than is necessary. He must be planning something awful, he just can't have chalked up THAT night to nervousness on my part, he can't, he can't, nobody is that nice.

26 February

Well, at least it's out now, I couldn't bear the tension a moment longer, I *had* to do something. I made the decision this morning when I realised I was grinding my teeth on the bus on the way to work, I was doing it loudly enough to elicit loud tusking from the person sitting next to me, at one point I seemed to be emitting a sort of low growl too, even the bag lady in front of me moved seats. I'd had enough of sleepless nights, so I marched into Andy's office, straight from the lift, without stopping to take my coat off or anything, and confronted him. I said, 'Look, I know you think I'm a hopeless wino and I know you thought I looked so revolting in the nude, well, semi-nude, that you are only being nice to me because you feel sorry for me and possibly also because I'm senior to you. Lovely Dan says you're gay, I don't think you are, but I *do* think you'd rather be that, than sleep with me so why can't you just come out with it instead of endlessly torturing me with all this being nice to me?'

Andy didn't say anything for a moment, but when he did, it was 'Could you give us a few minutes?' I was a bit thrown at first, then I saw that he wasn't talking to me but to New Secretary Sarah! She'd been in the room the whole time, taking dictation, not of my outburst, I hope, but from Andy – marvellous. Anyway, once she'd sidled her way out of there, carefully not looking me in the eye, Andy closed the door and said, 'I don't think you are a wino, I'm not being nice to you because I feel sorry for you, you are only technically senior to me, I don't think you look revolting in the nude, in fact quite the contrary, and who's Lovely Dan?' I nearly died, I wish I'd never said the thing about being senior to him, oh, I could kick myself. I didn't really take in anything else . . . I mean he was bound to say what he said, wasn't he? He could hardly have stood there, counting off the accusations one by one – 'That's yes to the you-foul-naked item, yes to the only being nice to you because I feel sorry for you, and yes to my not being homosexual but preferring it as option to having sex with you', could he?

A bit of a hiatus followed – well, I think he was just waiting for a response but I had other things to worry about. I was now more unhappy about having worn those suede, knee-high boots than anything else. What with the central heating in the office, they'd suddenly gone all tight and it felt like someone was pumping hot water into my calves. It was certainly very warm in Andy's office, maybe he's the sort of bloke that has the heat turned up so women will take their jackets off. Suddenly

I didn't feel so confident. When I'd come into the office it had been freezing outside and I felt a bit thin, like you do when it's cold, but now I felt all flustered and sweaty. My legs felt like I was standing in a cauldron of boiling lard, I just wanted to crawl out of there on my hands and knees, praying that he wouldn't see the boots. Eventually I decided to head him off – 'He's my best friend Sally's fiancé.' 'Who is?' Andy said (God, he's a bit slow on the uptake). 'Lovely Dan, you know, who thought you were gay, he's my best friend Sally's fiancé' – 'Oh' was all that Andy could manage. He'd probably noticed the excess flesh on my knees melting over the top of my boots by now. Just as I was going to make a run for it, Andy said, 'Can't we just forget about that night? I was a bit worse for wear too, let's have lunch next time, that might be easier.' Well, just when you think it's safe to go back in the water! He completely threw me again, I just don't know what to make of this relentless niceness, I don't seem to be programmed for dealing with somebody so straightforward. So, without thinking twice I'd agreed to lunch the Sunday after next – marvellous, so now all I've got is ten days to worry about what outfit looks casual, attractive *yet* plausible as something you'd wear for a weekend lunch.

Got home, having gone via the gym and done a really punishing class with the Nazi. I couldn't work out, for the life of me, what was going on – confronting Andy, going to the gym, grinding my teeth in public, snarling like an old hag at a teenager who pushed in at the bus stop, and then all was explained – my period's started. I must start keeping a proper chart of my cycle otherwise this out-of-body-aliens-have-possessed-me feeling is going to ambush me every time. Thing is, it's hard to recognise because PMT feels different every time – that's the subtlety of its power – never mind the atom bomb, scientists should really be focusing on capturing the level of destruction a woman feels every 28 days. I'm either screaming obscenities in the traffic, mulling over a selection of fantasy terminal diseases I've got so that Perfect Peter will be really sorry he left me, or ringing up Sally to see if having a bath is a good idea or not. I don't know whether the aggression or the indecision is worse – it took me 40 minutes to decide whether to watch *The Bill* or go over the conference schedule. By the time I'd kind of reached a decision *The Bill* was over and I felt so shit I ate a whole packet of Hob-Nobs – don't know what they were doing in the house anyway ... I wonder who put them there ... oh God, I think they were some of the shopping I'd done for Old Mrs M.

NB: Impress upon Old Mrs M. inadvisability of eating biscuits at her age ... alternatively (and perhaps more kindly) suggest that the more criminal style of foodstuffs are brought in by the Meals on Wheels crew – evidently I cannot be trusted to be alone with items of this nature.

NB: I do seem to have PMT a lot of the time, it's either premenstrual tension, DMT (during menstrual tension) or AMT (after menstrual tension). Maybe I should try not think-ing about it.

28 February

Need to shave my legs, but I don't want to tempt fate and look like I think I've got a reason to shave them ... I'll leave them.

1 March

There's been nothing much to report over the last couple of days. The evening my period started it goes without saying that I ate a Big Mac, large fries . . . yes, alright and a milk-shake . . . but I didn't finish that. Well, once I'd eaten the Hob-Nobs nothing seemed to matter any more – anyway, if you're already a packet of biscuits up you may as well go the whole hog.

NB: Do not go to the supermarket in the afternoon again. Saturday after 4 p.m. is evidently the time Sainsbury's open their doors to people in need of psychiatric care. I nearly came to blows with a man over the last pot of houmous and, menstruation notwithstanding, I do *not* think I was at fault – there was something decidedly manic about his determination to secure that Greek starter.

Hired a video with Sally, *Sleepless in Seattle*, Dan wouldn't watch it, he said it was too sloppy. Sally cried all the way through but I'm with Dan on this one, what sort of idiot obsesses about a man to that extent! The girl in that film had gone over every possible permutation of the relationship before it had even started – honestly! I was a bit pissed off with Sally actually, because after I told her what had happened with Andy she slapped an embargo on discussing possible motives for him asking me to lunch. All she would say was that he was obviously a really nice bloke and that I should take the invitation at face value. She also said, 'We never analysed every little thing that Perfect Peter did and he was a complete shit to you most of the time.' I don't need to scrutinise the minutiae of bad behaviour because I know where I am with that kind of carry-on. It's normal people being honest about how they feel *and*, what's more, liking me that panics and confuses me! That reminds me, I haven't heard from that therapy place yet ... maybe they don't think I'm neurotic enough.

2 March

Keith, my paragon-of-virtue-went-to-a-proper-university-not-just-a-business-college brother, came round for lunch today, hadn't seen him for a while. It was alright, except I made the mistake of complaining about Mum to him. I always forget that whenever I do, he always says something sanctimonious and really mature, like 'She's had a difficult time since Dad remarried, you should be more gentle with her' – as if she hasn't made my life living hell since I had the audacity and thoughtlessness to remain single after hitting 30. I wonder if an arranged marriage would keep Mum quiet – I could offer myself up to some decrepit Russian dissident, there are always loads of odd people looking for British passports. It was nice to see Keith, despite his annoying habit of seeing everything from everyone else's point of view. I did manage to get him to giggle about Jennifer's plans for Dad's sixtieth birthday party – the idea is that we all, that's including Bee and Kyle, have a meal on a boat on the Thames. 'Failing that ...' I said, 'we could just all wear T-shirts with NAFF IDEA printed across them.' I know Jennifer means well but how early '80s can you get? ... the only thing missing from her plan is Gareth Hunt. Keith wasn't very enthusiastic about the décor of my flat, he said it looked like the set of a kid's TV show. I explained that bold colours were 'in' now – he tried to make a connection between bold and brassy, which I resisted. Decided not to tell him about Andy because he'd probably have some really-mature-proper-university advice and then I'd be all out of sorts again. I did admit to having lied about a new boyfriend to Jennifer but, to my surprise, he thought that was quite funny and that I should keep it up. He even suggested that I take somebody along to Dad's birthday pretending that he was this new boyfriend. I think Keith made it a little too obvious, for my liking, that he thought there was no chance of there *actually* being a real new boyfriend by Dad's birthday and that a pretend one would be a hilarious diversion for him. As he was leaving, I asked him if he'd be bringing a girlfriend. He said, 'Jack . . . remember I'm forging ahead in my chosen profession, single and free from all ties, as is entirely appropriate for a young man in his 30s . . . whereas you are past your best, on the shelf and trying to cover this sad fact up by masquerading as a career woman.' I *think* he was teasing, but I'd need hallucinogenic drugs before I'd be able to see the funny side of paraphrasing Mum.

4 March

I'm getting quite bored of feeling guilty about not making daily entries . . . maybe I should make monthly or bi-monthly entries, summing up what's happened that month, putting in the most interesting bits . . . mmm, don't know – how would I decide what the best bits are? Best bits, that's a laugh, more like not-quite-so-banal-and-turgid-as-the-rest-of-my-life bits.

Had a summit meeting with Mr Bowyer today, just him

and me ... I was a bit worried Andy might feel all left out and pay me back by cancelling lunch – but I waited for Mr Bowyer to go into the meeting room first and I slipped in a couple of seconds afterwards by the other door, the one that can't be seen from Andy's office, so that he wouldn't think we were ganging up on him. Mr Bowyer said Carlo Pozzi and his colleagues were looking forward to the first conference (it's only about a month away now – 9 April, Glasgow) and that they were all very pleased with developments to date. He suggested I go up to Glasgow for one day, during the next couple of weeks, to finalise things, as it is important that this being the first one it goes off perfectly. He also said Andy should go along too. He's left it to me to tell Andy about this – oh God, how am I going to mention it to Andy without going puce? I know officially it's part of his job, the senior marketing person should obviously be there too, but I don't want him to think I asked for him to come along. Maybe I should send him a memo, that'd look quite nonchalant, wouldn't it? A quick, brisk, businesslike memo, casually informing him that we will be spending a day, alone, together ... perhaps something like—

MEMO
To: ~~Attractive New Andy~~ erm ... Andrew Canfield, Marketing Department
From: Jacqueline Pane, Senior Conference Organiser

RE: POZZI SERIES OF CONFERENCES

Further to meeting with Mr Bowyer of Senior Management, decision has been taken for myself and yourself to go alone to Glasgow for a day, just us two, together. Purpose – that we, as a team, working hand in hand, can together establish all arrangements are in place for 9 April. Possibility of overnight, not with me ... well, obviously *with* me, but separate hotel rooms, so, not *with* me in that sense. Should inform you that this decision was taken wholly and exclusively by Mr Bowyer and was nothing to do with me at all ... in fact, first I heard of it was at that meeting, which, by the way, you weren't excluded from *per se*, it's just that we had to go over other things too.

That's OK, isn't it? There might be a few too many references to being alone and a team, which he might take the wrong way, or rather the right way, but I don't want him to think I mean it the wrong way, the whole office must think I mean it the right way ... I'll make sure this memo gets circulated to all departments.

If I get New Secretary Sarah to re-type and deliver it it'll look like I'm so busy and unbothered by spending a whole day with him alone that I haven't even got the time to mention the trip to him in passing. Also that'll give me a chance to flaunt my lack of interest in Andy to her. I've hardly dared look at her since that attractive display I made of myself in his office. While she's in here, taking the memo, I'll drop into the conversation that I have an unusual kind of Tourette's syndrome – that's that tic, where you can't help yourself shouting out 'fuck' and 'arse' in public ... well, I'll say that I have the little-known version that makes you shout out completely fabricated accusations at people indiscriminately and that they are always directed at people you've got nothing to do with and have, in fact, no particular interest in. I'd better add that I'm telling her about my affliction in confidence, otherwise she might think it's common knowledge and mention it to Mr Bowyer, or Thin

Clare, or Andy. Mind you, it might be worth Andy thinking I've got that, because if we do have a relationship, or even if we don't, every time I have a hysterical fit about something I could say what I like and then blame it on the syndrome.

NB: Ask Lovely Dan which of the following is less attractive in a PNG (Potential New Girlfriend):- a) an unpredictable speech defect or b) someone whose best friend's boyfriend thinks you're gay.

5 March

Mr Bowyer popped in to tell me he'd got his secretary to organise the tickets for Glasgow for the 26th of this month. I didn't tell him I hadn't told Andy about it yet, I must do something about that. I'm terrified of facing New Sec. Sarah – she's fairly timid but what if she's one of those people you're always hearing about with inner strength? I'll dictate the memo tomorrow just before I have to leave.

Sally came to meet me for lunch – she wasn't mad keen on the speech defect idea, at first, but she did admit it had enormous potential for the future. Sally often takes some talking round, she's all for that 'be loved for who you are and not what you think you should be' lark. I really have my work cut out sometimes, making her see how difficult that can be if you are in the middle of a self-discovery journey, but fancy someone before you've arrived at your destination. She and Lovely Dan met long before either of them had a clue who they were. I think it's easier that way round because you can both sort of make it up as you go along and then stop the other person discovering a 'self' you don't like.

8 March

I haven't written anything for the last couple of days because I've decided not to get into a hysterical flap about lunch with Andy tomorrow and if I try and think about anything else it just makes me think about the lunch so I have tried to completely empty my brain since my last entry, which is quite a good way to approach a date, I believe. Wait a minute, you're supposed to have an open mind, not an empty one – what if I've turned all vacant-looking?

Great news – letter arrived from that therapy place, they've offered me an assessment appointment on 1 April ... is that their idea of a joke? That's fab because it'll be before Dad's birthday and the first conference so I can get them to tell me how to be at both those functions. Mmmm, 'assessment' – that sounds a bit ominous. According to the book I've got, you have a few initial 'assessments' then they 'place' you with a counsellor or therapist they think will suit you. Bloody hell, that means I'll have to keep pretending to be really neurotic all the way through the assessment if I want to get a top-drawer therapist.

9 March

Post-lunch-with-Andy entry. Wore a T-shirt, long cardigan,

which I'd checked completely covered my bum from all angles, and a long skirt ... I had been going to wear those M&S trousers but I couldn't run the risk of Andy seeing the size 16 label inside them.

NB: Buy some size 8 clothes, cut the labels out and sew them in my real clothes, for future leaving-lying-around-on-the-floor purpose.

The cardigan was very expensive but I think the T-shirt made it look like I wasn't wearing the costliest item in my wardrobe and had just thrown something on in a very Sunday-ish, casual way.

My heart sank when he suggested we meet at one of those French cafés – I always feel like a complete failure if I'm not reading *Le Monde* cover to cover with a half-drunk espresso in front of me. We arrived at exactly the same time, which was good, because I didn't have time to worry about who looked the least cool, etc. After we'd ordered the food, Andy said, 'Listen, I'd like to clear up the events of our dinner. You were in no state to know what you were doing, so I just put you to bed and left it at that ... I was sort of expecting you to ring the next day and when you didn't, I assumed you weren't interested in me, but that's behind us now and here we are.' Mercifully, the restaurant had those long menus that fold out into three sections, so I held that up in front of my face from the moment he uttered the word 'dinner'. I was paralysed with embarrassment and confusion – I had no idea what to say. His straightforwardness made me feel all nude and awkward. I ended up not really responding at all and the first thing I did manage to get out was the observation that the only real difference between *tarte aux pommes* and *tarte tatin* appears to be that one is cooked upside down and the other is not – and I even got that off the menu.

Despite my chronic inability to behave like an adult in front of Andy, we did have a nice time together. We went for a walk after lunch, which I didn't really like because I never know *how* to walk with someone I fancy. Do you look at him while you're walking, showing him that you're interested in what he's saying – in which case, you run the risk of tripping up? Do you look at where you're walking, making appropriate interjections while he's talking, to show him you're listening – in which case, you run the risk of looking like you can't walk and talk at the same time? Do you do a bit of both, mixing both disciplines – looking at him and the path – in which case, you run the risk of getting very dizzy and losing your balance? I couldn't decide so I just did a little bit of everything but I'm sure it would have looked better if I'd stuck to one style of walking. Going for a walk with someone you fancy is actually very hard work.

NB: Cover 'Ways to Walk with a PNB' when I write my self-help book.

As we were parting company, Andy said he was looking forward to the day trip to Glasgow. It appears that Bowyer's secretary had mentioned it to him before I'd got round to it – copper-bottomed proof that there is a God. Now I won't have to resort to elaborate lies about speech problems ... might keep that one behind my ear for another time, though, it's quite a goodie.

When I got home there was a message from Sally asking me to ring her as soon as I got home to let her know all about the lunch. As I was playing the answermachine back it suddenly occurred to me – if I can hear Downstairs Man and the Foghorn's episodes of wild abandon, then he can surely hear stuff that goes on in my flat? As I'm currently unencumbered by activities of that nature, I'm OK for now, but it'd probably be quite therapeutic and healthy to prepare for a brighter, sexually active, future. Next time he's out, get

Sally to come round and stand by his front door, I'll go into my flat, groan and mutter a few saucy things (it's been so long since I had sex, I'll probably have to read it out of *Marie Claire*) and then Sal can tell me what she could hear. At least, I don't have to worry about Old Mrs M. – she's so deaf, I could fell a tree in my living room and she wouldn't hear. I was feeling quite positive about the date with Andy until Sally asked if we'd kissed. You don't kiss at lunch-time, do you? Oh, what did Sally have to go and ask that for? Now I'm going to spend all night wondering why he didn't kiss me. I'm sort of glad he didn't, though, because my skin looks much worse up close in the day than it does at night and also I feel a bit of a pranny closing my eyes to kiss during the daytime.

11 March

Nothing much to report, been in a mad spin at work, decided to completely tidy up my office and desk, but ended up just moving things about on it. Still a different layout makes it look like I'm in control – oh, did get rid of that bright pink plastic pen and paper-clips desk organiser thing. I hate those things, the only thing they can be relied upon to do is sabotage a good manicure. The pens all leak into them and then when you're scrabbling around for a paper clip or file binder you get a nail full of Biro innards instead. Andy is still keeping up his niceness – I wonder what his childhood was like, maybe he was brought up by Mary Poppins.

Been to the gym every day since Sunday. It's the cellulite away-day in a couple of days and I don't want to be taken aside by the workshop leader and told that I'm beyond redemption and asked to leave ... or worse asked if I've considered amputation.

13 March

Had a lunch with Andy and Thin Clare today. I hardly need say that it wasn't my idea. I was sitting in the canteen eating a salad (I'd had a couple of sandwiches in the lavs around twelve, so that I'd look slim having just a salad in front of everyone else). I'd brought some notes up from my office with me to make sure I looked preoccupied, if anyone noticed I was sitting alone. Anyway, without planning it I actually was completely engrossed in reading them when I heard Thin Clare and Andy ask if they could join me. Andy asked me if the salad was all I was having and before I could say anything, Thin Clare said, 'Oh, she hardly ever eats a thing, I don't know how she manages.' BUGGER OFF AND DIE, THIN CLARE! The subtext, no, not even the subtext, more like the in-your-face message, was perfectly clear to me. I knew very well what she was really saying – 'Oh, don't be fooled by the salad, it's true that she hardly ever eats a thing, but that's only in front of people. You see, behind closed doors she must be stuffing her face night and day with high-fat, high-calorie foods that she is, understandably, too ashamed to eat in front of healthy, clean-living individuals such as ourselves. And bearing in mind that she is not exactly a rake, like me for example, then it is only right and proper that she keeps her filthy eating habits to herself and spares others the foul sight of her troughing away like a wild boar grovelling for truffles.' The only thing that kept me from fainting with shame right there and then was the knowledge that I hadn't had a pudding or a starter when Andy and I had lunch together. Still, it felt like my trusty eat-enjoyable-food-alone-and-virtuous-food-in-front-of-witnesses cover had been blown right out of the water. I was weak with embarrassment, Thin Clare might as well have projected a hologram on to the canteen wall of what my breasts and stomach look like when I'm sitting up in the bath. I had to act quickly, before Andy started to make a list in his head of everything I'd ever eaten in front of him. I quickly dropped my fork, pushed the salad away with a contemptuous gesture, made a point of mentioning I was full and raced out of there saying that I had to get on with some urgent work.

14 March

There's a possibility that I might have slightly overreacted yesterday. Thin Clare came up to me today and said that she and Andy were sorry for interrupting me in the canteen when I'd obviously wanted to be alone. Either she's covering herself or she genuinely hasn't realised how fat I really am ... can't be sure at this stage. It made me bristle, though, her apologising for 'her and Andy' like that, as if it's understood that they are 'as one' and share all human sentiments and together have collective regret. However, it is certainly better if they think I'm a bad-tempered and unsociable person than a greedy, piggy one.

Noted that New Secretary Sarah was eating a KitKat at teatime – I wonder what it's like to be able to eat something like that in an office filled with people and not be thinking everyone's either pitying you or laughing at you.

16 March

Wow! Just come back from the cellulite away-day. It was fantastic. I really do believe there is life without cellulite now. It's going to take a lot of hard work and commitment but it can be done – you just have to believe. We all met up in the mosque hall at 11.30 yesterday morning. There were about 20 of us and a group leader (who, I must admit, didn't look like she was a complete stranger to cellulite even now – at least she's started the good fight, I suppose). We were each given the 'Learning to Live without Cellulite' starter pack ... well, actually you had to pay extra for it. I was a bit annoyed because I'd thought the £95 plus VAT the day'd cost (should have been £95 plus FAT, hah, hah!) covered all expenses. Apparently it's all part of the continuing regime and you do get to take the pack home with you. This very helpful list came with it:

LEARNING TO LIVE WITHOUT CELLULITE – THE MANTRA:

1. Cellulite is not a disease.
2. Cellulite is an illness, it is not terminal and can be cured.
3. Cellulite is hereditary.
4. Cellulite spreads. If not eradicated, it will cover most of your body within a few years, excepting feet and lips.
5. Successful people do not have cellulite. Cellulite can and will ruin your life.
6. Cellulite will take over if you let it – together we can fight it.

You're supposed to stick that up on your fridge or in your bathroom – someplace where you'll see it every day. Seems like quite a good idea but a bit dangerous. What if some joker like the Cheeky Window Cleaner sees it and decides to shout out, while he's standing on the outside ledge, 'Suffer from cellulite do you, then, love? The wife's got that, disgusting, ain't it?' Safer to put it on the fridge and camouflage it with some punishing, very worthy diet sheet.

After we'd all paid for our kits, we all sort of milled around, reading the checklist, and looking through our packs which consisted of some lotions, a couple of jars of dried leaves and what looked like a medieval oven glove. Then the leader asked us to form a circle and to say our names, sticking to first names only – for the sake of anonymity. When everyone had introduced themselves, the leader asked us to, one by one, stand up and say where we had cellulite and what our fears were about it. I was ready to leave at that point but some foolish woman owned up, almost immediately, to having it practically everywhere except her face and hands, so I felt alright about staying. There were loads of women there who had it in all the same locations as me and they were happily admitting it left right and centre – it became a bit of a cellulite-fest. I decided I could be economical when it came to my confession. When it was my turn, I stood up and admitted to having a trace of it on the tops of my thighs. Gosh, the look of envy on the others' faces – it was worth the treachery. We then broke for lunch – except there was nothing to eat, obviously. I had begun to wonder whether fatty cells and their implications could be sustained as the sole topic of discussion for a whole day. But it turned out it was more of a support group than a practical – I suppose the theory is as important as the practice. For the rest of the day everyone just sat around sharing their cellulitey experiences. One woman,

Julia, talked very frankly about the years she'd spent trying to deny she'd got it. She told us about how she'd constructed a life never looking in mirrors and wearing kaftans. Until one day she'd finally had to face it, when her little boy had asked her husband, 'Why does my mummy have tiny moon craters that look like orange peel all over her bottom and legs?' The leader then said we could all conquer it and everyone whooped and yelled and applauded. I kept fairly quiet throughout the day – I had to distance myself from those chronic cellulite sufferers, establishing myself as someone who had it under control and knew how to handle it.

The day ended with the leader taking us through the starter pack. Apparently we have to pummel our problem areas with the medieval oven glove three times a day – three times a day! My problem areas are so widespread, I'll have to consider going part time at work if I'm going to stick to this regime. With the dried leaves you make two sorts of compresses – one hot and one cold. Mercifully, that's only once a day but the bloody lotions have to be applied three times a day – in the morning, during the day and last thing at night. Oh, I can just see the fun I'm going to have – now I've got to cram down two sandwiches *and* get my entire kit off to apply the lotions – and that's all during my lunch-hour.

Just popped over to Mrs M.'s, she was watching *The Good Sex Guide* – that's quite a good programme for her, because even if you weren't deaf, you'd only ever want to look at the screen and not hear what they were saying. When I told her about my away-day, she asked what cellulite was!! God, it must have been brilliant having sex in the old days – your husband never expected to see you in the nude – ever. In fact I don't think anybody expected to see anybody in the nude, no wonder they didn't know what cellulite was. Cellulite has probably only been invented since the sexual revolution.

18 March

Found a good place for the mantra list – on the underside of the crisper drawer in the fridge. I have to lie down on the kitchen floor to read it, not hugely convenient but at least no one else will see it there.

19 March

One week today, one week today – one week today I go to Glasgow with Andy.

NB: Do not think about trip with Andy too much, maximum allowance – once an hour.

22 March

I couldn't face the gym today – I won't eat anything for the rest of the weekend to make up for it.

I happened to be browsing through an atlas and noticed that Glasgow is only a few miles north of Gretna Green – that's the place where you can get married without a licence or any notice.

NB: Do not mention scenic drive, taking in the Gretna area – Andy might feel pressured into proposing.

23 March

Rang Mum – I'd woken up realising that fate might pay me back for never calling her and make the plane to Glasgow crash. Told her I was coming up for the first weekend in May, added more points to my don't-deserve-to-die-in-a-plane-crash-because-I have-done-a-good-thing by not reacting when she said, 'I suppose if you weren't doing a conference in Birmingham, I wouldn't be getting this visit.' Told her I'd had lunch with Keith, which was a mistake – of course he'd pipped me to the post with this information having characteristically rung Mum long before me. I became desperate to offer her up a titbit that couldn't lead into criticism of me, so I told her about Jennifer's naff plans for Dad's birthday. Oh, vitriol akimbo – she was off and running. 'That woman doesn't know your father at all, when we were together we always hated activities masquerading as dinners. I'd rather have my eyes gouged out with hot knives than eat on a boat, blah, blah, blah . . .'

NB: Jennifer is a most useful human shield when wishing to deflect Mum's offensives on self.

24 March

I don't believe it, I simply cannot believe my luck, I am evidently destined to remain hairy and single for the rest of my days. I've just realised my period is starting any day now – it must be, there's no other explanation for not being able to get into my black-and-grey wraparound skirt. What the hell is it doing *not* wrapping around – that's what those bloody skirts do, they wrap around, that's their job, they have no purpose in life other than to wrap around.

I got up this morning, opened the fridge, lay on the floor, read my cellulite mantra, trounced my thighs with the medieval oven glove until I nearly drew blood and then started my getting dressed regime. As usual, I'd organised what I was going to wear last thing before I'd gone to bed. I've found that I only ever sleep properly if I know how I'm going to be kitted out the next day (have also found that it is crucial to take entire wardrobe when going out of town). Otherwise I lie awake all night worrying about having to get ready in a hurry and not noticing that my tights are on the wrong way round, or that my shoes make me look old and spinstery, or that a certain blouse makes me look mad.

Foolishly I'd thought of this skirt as a trusted ally and not tried on my chosen outfit last night, as I would normally. My whole existence was thrown into question – the skirt just would not wrap around. The success of my entire day lay squarely on the wearing of that skirt. It's my absolute best skirt-for-looking-slim-in-when-walking. I had a meeting on the eighth floor, which involves traversing the length of the office to get to the back lift, and I'd also scheduled some 'walking past Andy's office in a casual fashion'. The ends of the skirt were still meeting, but one section of the skirt is supposed to overlap the other bit – obviously, otherwise it wouldn't be a wraparound, it would be more like one of those flaps African tribesmen wear that cover their behinds but leave their genitalia on display. In a crisis, I admit, I would rather have my fanny on display than my bottom, any day of the week – natch – but this wasn't that kind of a crisis. Sure, if someone held a gun to my head and offered me a smallish piece of material saying 'Cover either your bum or your fanny with this' then I'd go for the bum every time, hands down, no question, but this wasn't a life-or-death situation, it was more important than that. This skirt normally fulfils its job description – as a bloody wraparound skirt – but, now, apparently it was on strike. No negotiations, no warning, no arbitration, it had just downed tools, and taken a totally non-cooperative stand. This skirt was my friend, I trusted it, I knew where I stood with it, it was one of the few things in my life I'd ever really loved. Why had it given up on me now – just when I needed it most? Why, oh why wouldn't it meet? I was still able do it up but the overlap bits were resolutely refusing to meet from halfway down my stomach onwards – revealing a sort of pyramid of flesh. I thought about Sellotaping the sides to each other all the way to the hem, but decided against that, when I realised that the Sellotape would probably stick to my tights as well and pull them off, or at least ladder them into shreds.

I didn't know what to do. I called work to say I was going to be late, I had to have time to think and fast. I rang Sally (thankfully she's recently become unemployed). Her first suggestion was to drop the 'walking past Andy's office in a casual fashion' item from my agenda. I was so wound up, I lost my temper with her. 'Obviously that's out of the window, now that I can't get into my looking-slim-in-walking-skirt, you bloody moron, but I still have to go to that meeting. Now, think, do I stick to last night's line-up of clothes, only substituting the rebel skirt for that unbelievably expensive black skirt I got to cheer myself up when I broke up with Perfect Peter but hardly ever wear now? Or do I go for the navy blue suit with the knee-length skirt that looks quite good but I can't breathe or bend over in?'

Sally redeemed herself and came to an immediate tough, no-nonsense decision – 'Stick to last night's outfit because that's been worked out properly, go for that black skirt and may the force be with you.' I just managed to get to the office in time for the meeting. Luckily nobody seemed to notice that I didn't have my planned skirt on. I felt slightly self-conscious for the rest of the day, though. That I've-got-something-on-that-I-obviously-hardly-ever-wear-so-it-probably-makes-me-look-all-pathetic-and-like-I'm-making-a-special-effort feeling haunted me all day. You know that feeling you used to get when you wore party shoes when you were a child. Actually, I still get that feeling when I wear new shoes to a party now ... and not just to a party ... and not just new shoes ... new anything makes me feel like that. I usually wear new things round my flat, slouching in front of the TV, or wiping down the surfaces in the kitchen, before I'll put them on to go outside – in front of people. I don't want the whole world looking at me and thinking, 'Oh look at you, all keen and desperate, spending money on new clothes, like you're worth it, HAH!'

NB: Ask Mrs M. if she can sew in a temporary insert into offending wraparound skirt ... mmm, might look a bit circa '72.

25 March

It's Glasgow tomorrow, och aye the noo! ... is that how you spell noo? What is a noo ... perhaps I'll find out in Glasgow.

Andy suggested picking me up in a cab on the way to the airport but I said I'd see him there ... it's nerve-racking enough spending the whole day with him, I'm not going to prolong the agony any more than I have to.

27 March

Oh, my word, you are never going to believe what happened
... I can't believe it. Glasgow was a disaster – a complete,
sell-out, top-of-the-range flop. I'd better start at the beginning.
I've only just got back and I don't suppose I can ring Sally,
it's 2 a.m., I mean I know she's unemployed but she still
needs to sleep. As arranged, Andy and I met at the Scot
Air check-in desk and as we were sorting out our tickets
and stuff – guess who turns up? Carlo Pozzi! I had no
idea he was coming, Mr Bowyer hadn't mentioned anything
about it. Anyway, Carlo pitches up, gives Andy a peculiar look
and says to me, 'I thought you'd be doing this trip on your
own, you're only going for the day, to check on last-minute
arrangements, aren't you?' Before I could reply, Andy, who
had become very agitated (I think he may be funny about
flying or something because he really looked unhappy), said,
'It was felt that someone from marketing ought to go as well,
to check things from that angle.' I don't think Carlo can have
heard him, because he just completely ignored him and said to
me, 'I was looking forward to spending time with you, I have
some clients I need to see near Glasgow, so when I heard you
were going up for the day I thought we could travel together
and maybe have dinner this evening.'

GOD, and all this time I'd thought he was after Thin Clare
... how could I have been so dim? I can't believe I didn't
see it before. It's so obvious – he's after Andy, he's obviously
gay, he must be – good-looking, beautifully dressed and really
nice to women ... it all adds up. All that paying attention to
me stuff, at that first meeting, the phoning me up, etc. – it
wasn't to get Thin Clare's attention, it was for Andy's benefit!
I was suddenly panic-stricken that I might be in the way. The

thing is, I'm pretty sure Andy isn't gay, despite what Lovely Dan says. Unless, oh dear, unless I've been really slow on the uptake and Andy is gay and has been giving Carlo those secret signals that only people who fancy each other pick up on (I'm not too familiar with what those signals actually are, I think my receiver may be a bit faulty).

I didn't know what to do in case they wanted to be with each other but needed me as a decoy kind of thing, to make it look respectable, or whether Andy, if he wasn't gay, didn't want to be alone with Carlo in case he jumped on him. I sat between them on the plane, so that everything looked normal. The flight was quite uncomfortable because they didn't seem to want to talk to each other, so I was trying to keep two different conversations bubbling at once. I got a bit flustered at one point and mixed up who I was talking to about what and told Andy that I'd never been to Venice, although our topic of conversation had been the possibility of designated parking spaces at work. I hope he doesn't think I'm mad.

Once we got to Glasgow I decided I'd better make myself scarce and get on with checking things at the conference centre, so when Carlo mentioned dinner at some restaurant he knew I suggested that we all meet up there. This time both Andy and Carlo looked a bit askance. I had no idea what was going on now – I was just trying to make things easier, I didn't want to be the spare lemon at the wedding . . . it isn't lemon, is it? . . . oh, never mind, I just didn't want to be responsible for mucking things up. Andy and I went off to the conference centre where everything went smoothly. Andy was strangely silent most of the day, though – I wondered if he was cross with me, because I'd spoilt his evening with Carlo, but he hadn't known Carlo was coming up either, I don't think. I suppose he could just have been silent because he couldn't think of anything to say to me. The flight had been a bit turbulent, it could just have been that.

We all met up in the evening at this very nice restaurant but dinner was very hard work. Carlo kept lapsing into Italian, presumably because he's quite sexy when he speaks his native tongue and wanted Andy to see him at his best. I didn't want to talk Italian back in case Andy thought I was showing off, but I couldn't be rude to our big client, so I tried responding half in Italian and half in English, which I think only served to make me completely unintelligible to both of them. Again, Andy didn't say much at all, but I think that's because he must have been dreading the flight back. Neither of them spoke to the other throughout dinner, so they definitely fancy each other. I was so nervous that I was either a gooseberry coming between them or a chaperone for Andy that I talked sixteen to the dozen for most of the meal anyway. Three people is not a great number for any gathering, I've decided, I wasn't able to relax at all. God knows how people go in for threesomes, dinner with two people who aren't talking to each other is bad enough, what on earth can it be like if you're all trying to reach a simultaneous climax and two of them won't talk to each other!

I was so worn out by the effort of trying to work out what was going on that I fell asleep on the flight back . . . well, only half asleep, I wasn't going to run the risk of my head bobbing from side to side. There is nothing more humiliating than falling asleep sitting up, when your head sort of lolls slowly forward until your chin is folded up on your chest, then someone moves and you whiplash your head back again, all the time asleep, then it stays like that for a few seconds, until the imitation of Katharine Hepburn in *On Golden Pond* starts all over again. Your head starts nodding forward to a distinct rhythm – back a bit, forward a bit, back, back, forward, forward, until this time, instead of ending up on your chest, it ends up on the shoulder of the stranger sitting next to you, and then you're both stuck. He daren't move because he's British and doesn't want to bring attention to himself, ignoring the fact that the entire carriage, cabin, whatever, is transfixed by the spectacle you've made of yourself and is on the edge of their seats, waiting, as one, for the gloriously undignified moment your mouth opens ever so slightly and the saliva starts drip, drip, dripping in slow motion on to the stranger's newspaper. Oh no, that wasn't going to happen to me, not now, not ever. I wasn't going to let myself become the freak floor show for bored travellers. I was going to stay awake if it killed me, flanked, as I was, by the object of my desire and one of my company's biggest clients.

Homosexuals or not, they'd probably still enjoy the sight of my head lolling about like one of those dogs you see in the back of cars – anybody would, I laugh when it's someone else.

I got home completely depressed – my big day out/chance of a lifetime with Andy ruined. If Andy turns out to be gay then what does that say about me? It says, as usual, that I can't tell the difference between a complex social nuance and a loaf of bread.

NB: No Tampax in the house and my period's just started, I'll have to improvise with half a lavatory roll and an old pair of pants – perfect end to a beautiful day.

30 March

Haven't felt much like writing in the last few days . . . haven't felt much like breathing actually, but at least you can do that without too much effort and you don't have to think about it.

Avoided Andy at work, couldn't face the sight of him mincing down the corridor. To be fair he doesn't mince, well, he didn't, as far as I know, but what if I just hadn't noticed it before, or now I think he is mincing, but he isn't really?

Haven't been sticking very rigidly to my 'Living without Cellulite' regime. The last time I lay down to read the mantra, I got my hair caught on the bottom of the fridge and nearly scalped myself when I stood up ... might have to find a different place to put it. It won't really matter if I'm covered head to foot in the stuff if Andy turns out to be 'not as other men,' though, will it?

Lucky I'm feeling so foul, it'll ensure that I'm really depressed and seem neurotic for my therapy assessment tomorrow. Can't decide whether to wear something that makes me look really sad and low-self-esteemy, so that the assessor really pities me and makes sure I get a great therapist, or something nice that I look alright in. If I wear something sad, I'll have to change before I go on to work, but that's not necessarily a problem. The main thing, for this occasion, is to pick the outfit that makes me look mad.

NB: Think I'll wear the jeans, then the therapist will know what I'm talking about when I explain that I only ever wear them to upset my dad. On second thoughts, I'll wear my work outfit and change into the mad gear in the loos when I get there, in case anyone sees me on the way.

1 April

Today is the first day of the rest of my life – new, improved, fabulous life the therapy way.

I set off really early for my appointment. I was terrified about being late and having to waste half the session talking about what being late meant, so I ended up arriving at the clinic before it had opened. I flirted with the idea of waiting on the entrance steps to make me look extra desperate but realised that the only person who'd be likely to find me there was the cleaner, so I waited in a café round the corner. It was slightly uncomfortable in there, because the old Greek woman who ran the place gave me a look, when she gave me my coffee, like she was thinking, 'Here we go, another one of those nutters who thinks that place round the corner has got the answers.' Seven cappuccinos later I went to the clinic with ten minutes to go until I was going to be shown the light.

By this time I actually really needed to go to the loo, so I didn't have to worry about the receptionist wondering what I was doing going to the loo when I'd only just arrived. I had a pee (honestly, I don't need to put that kind of detail into my diary!) ... I changed into my jeans and went back into the waiting area. I don't think the receptionist noticed I'd changed clothes, in fact it's unlikely that she'd have noticed if I'd started sawing my head off with a blunt butter knife – she completely ignored me. I expect people who work in those places are trained not to ever look at anybody, in case that person has come in for paranoia or guilt – one of those states of mind that makes people think other people are thinking all sorts of awful things about them when they're not.

Anyway, I sat down and started getting cold feet, I mean, I really only wanted to talk about how awful my parents are and get confirmation that everything is their fault. OK, and maybe slag off the odd thin person now and again – not Thin Clare ... I've decided she's alright now and, anyway, strictly speaking, it's not her fault that she's thin. As the minutes crawled agonisingly slowly by, it dawned on me that you're probably not allowed to give the therapist a list of topics that you will and won't talk about. If I tried to do that, they'd start doing that irritating thing of making you talk about the one thing you don't want to talk about, and you'd end up either sulking or giving monosyllabic answers between gritted teeth – my normal response when Mum questions me about men I've met recently and what plans I've laid to pique their interest.

Anyway, on the dot of 10 a.m. (they must spend half their working day synchronising the clocks in that place) a woman popped her head out of a door along the corridor and called out my name. I shuffled along the hall and entered a poky little brown room – it looked like it had been decorated with silt, I suppose that's their idea of a neutral colour. Sitting in an armchair opposite a much more uncomfortable-looking empty chair was a very fat woman!! I was completely thrown, I didn't know what to do. A fat therapist! How could a therapist be fat and good at her job? If she was any good, she wouldn't be fat – right? That'd be like a divorced marriage guidance counsellor, or a right-wing Labour MP . . . oh, there are quite a lot of those, aren't there . . . well, that's different, but you know what I mean.

She was so large that she sort of fitted right into the armchair, it looked as if the armchair might actually be part of her body (probably quite useful for a therapist – seeing as they mainly sit around all day).

I didn't know whether to tell her up front that her being fat was a shock to me or whether just to pretend not to have noticed her size (HAH!) and talk about myself, the size of my bum, the whole cellulite issue, etc. and just keep my fingers crossed that she wouldn't think I was criticising her. While I was trying to decide what to say I noticed that fifteen minutes had already gone by! Isn't she ever going to utter? Is this some sort of test? Is the first one to speak a cissy? After what seemed like hours, she finally spoke. She had a very soothing, gentle way of speaking which I liked. She asked what particular areas of concern had led me to consider therapy. Straight away, I decided she was a bit thick . . . I mean, there I was sitting in a pair of jeans. I would have thought a quick glance at the way I look in them makes it perfectly obvious why I need therapy! There was another hiatus while I contemplated flouncing out with a contemptuous look but I decided against that when I realised I might look like I'd got aggression problems too. Eventually I explained that I didn't really know why I was there but I was hoping that they'd be able to point out my main problem areas and then help me get rid of them. I mean, that's sort of it in a nutshell, isn't it?

I could simply have cut to the chase and said, 'Well, I've got a fat bum and it rules my life' but I was terrified she'd say, 'Yes, I can see how it would, especially if you wear those jeans a lot.' And if she'd said something like that, I couldn't really have said, 'Look who's talking, lard arse' because that would open up a whole other can of worms about my defensiveness or something else equally infuriating and not really relevant because it would have been she that would have started it but I'd end up looking like the one who was at fault.

After that we both sat there in silence for a bit longer, me willing her to notice the vast expanse of my denim-clad thighs and say something like, 'Do you have concerns about weight?' – but she didn't.

Another annoying thing about therapy is that I think you're supposed to take responsibility for identifying your own problems! Great, next they'll try and formulate an argument that absolves my parents of all blame! Suddenly I noticed there were only fifteen minutes left and my life was nowhere near sorted – I had to reveal something! I decided to give her something juicy – it had to be good otherwise she might not see me again. So I told her that I used to sleep with people I didn't really fancy to get them to like me but that it didn't really happen any more because I'd lost faith that free sex with me would be something that would necessarily make people like me. Yet again, she missed the point! She seemed to think the thing to focus on was the whole having-sex-with-people-just-to-make-them-like-me thing, when quite clearly the issue to discuss was why I'd lost faith that it would work! I mean, everybody sleeps with people they don't really fancy to be popular ... it's just not everybody loses confidence in it working. I mean, in the old days, I'd have had sex with Andy on his first day with the company – in the stockroom before he'd got his coat off – secure in the knowledge he'd adore me for it. Nowadays, I'd just fear it would put him off the stockroom (and me) for life.

Just as I was muscling up to give her another tasty morsel she stood up and said, 'That's all we have time for today, perhaps you'd like to come back at the same time next week when we can talk further.' Oh, yeah, can't wait, more exchanges at the speed of lightning. I'll probably end up going there in hot pants and a boob tube in an effort to get her to notice what the main 'issue' is. I might not go back next week – that'll show her ... then she'll be sorry she didn't come up with a few more insights.

NB: Avoid conviction that non-appearance of self results in disappointment for others – reverse is probably more accurate.

8 April

Don't know what I'm doing going to see that woman again.

It's the first one of the Pozzi conferences in Glasgow tomorrow and I'm flying up there first thing. I've got better things to do with my time than spoon-feed an overweight therapist who wouldn't recognise an 'issue' if it sat on her face!

I don't think I like this new discipline of only writing once a week but I've got to stick to it . . . not really sure why, but I suppose I'd better stick to things once I've decided that I should do them, no? Things have been hotting up so much in the countdown to tomorrow at work that I've barely talked to Andy since the 'love that dare not speak its name' trip to Glasgow. I did note that he was wearing a salmon-pink shirt the other day – so now I'm even more confused! I mean how can you know, without asking straight out? What if Andy doesn't know he's gay until I 'out' him? I've already got away with one outburst of accusations, I'm not sure I could justify another tirade, even if it does turn out that he's got all Judy Garland's records.

Saw Downstairs Man on the way out this morning, realised my return dinner invitation was hideously overdue, so I invited him for the 19th. I've got to do it some time, this weekend's too soon and it may as well be before I go up to Mum's. Hey, I've got an idea, I could arrange to have some electrolysis for the following weekend and make it a hat-trick of hellish Saturdays.

Needless to say, nothing much was resolved in the therapy session. I was wearing the same jeans but belted this time with a T-shirt tucked in and she *still* didn't bring up weight. Maybe I should have brought it up, but I don't want to in case she doesn't think I'm fat in comparison to her and gets all uppity about who's got the most right to be worried about their fatness. On reflection – I don't suppose we're in competition, are we? Her fatness shouldn't have anything to do with mine, really. Except that I've just got a bit of a problem taking how-to-improve-your-life advice from someone who's at least twice my body weight . . . maybe it's just me. Maybe I fixate on weight in a way that nobody else does . . . nah, that can't be it, that'd make me a paranoiac. Next time I must try and put her size out of my mind – I could try lying down on the couch and then I won't be able to see her, that might be an idea.

10 April

I know I'm not supposed to write anything until next Tuesday after therapy but we did the first of the Pozzi conferences yesterday and I can't wait until next week. I think the conference went really well. There was a hideous moment at the beginning when I got up to welcome everybody – the podium was a wooden platform which creaked really noisily as I walked towards the microphone, and I was completely thrown. I stood there, speechless, staring at a sea of faces, and realised that everyone present had one shared thought – 'She must weigh a ton to make a solid structure like that groan so loudly.' I quickly regained my composure when it was clear no one was actually going to shout this out loud. The whole day was pretty hectic, I didn't get a moment to sit down once – just as well because I'd worn the dark red suit that I can't sit down in anyway. Actually I can barely walk in it but it squishes everything in pretty effectively so it's a favourite. At the end of the day Carlo came up to me, full of compliments on how well the day had gone, he kept looking like he was about to say something else, like he was trying to tell me something . . . I don't know what. I'd prefer our relationship to stay strictly professional – I do not fancy being the one to whom he pours out his feelings for Andy ... or any other man, for that matter.

NB: In future maintain a cool but polite manner at all times with Carlo, or I'll end up being the pig in the middle – how appropriate.

Anyway, the important thing is that the conference went well and that I didn't have to take off my jacket. A few people mentioned that they thought it was a bit cold in the hall but I said the venue was having problems with the central heating. They weren't really having problems with it but if it'd got too warm in there then it might have looked peculiar that I'd kept my jacket on the whole time, so I'd deliberately kept the thermostat fairly low throughout the day.

15 April

Therapy session again today. I had to get to work quickly afterwards so I didn't have time to do the whole can't-you-see-how-fat-I-am-in-this? thing. I just wore what I was wearing for work. She made no comment about my appearance again. Maybe she's waiting until she thinks I'm ready to discuss it, maybe she has thought, 'God, she should never wear jeans again' but is biding her time before she broaches such an explosive subject. I told her a bit about Perfect Peter and how he'd moved to New York, she asked what my definition of perfect was and I said anyone who didn't want me. Ooops, I didn't really mean to say that, I mean that makes me sound really pathetic and not very sorted out. But afterwards I was really glad I'd said it because it probably notches me up a few more points towards the mark you need to qualify for a really good therapist. God, I can't wait to move on to the proper therapist. At the end of the session she asked me to make a list of all my good points and stick it up somewhere I'd see it every day. It's going to get pretty crowded under my fridge.

MY GOOD POINTS:

~~Nose~~
Erm . . . my feet? Not really, because of that long second toe next to the big one on my left foot.

Eyes, yes, eyes, they're quite good, aren't they? Quite big and brown – well, apart from the left one that has that tiny green splodge slightly to the left of the iris, you can only see it when I tilt my head back towards the light, but still, it's a flaw. And anyway my eyelashes aren't long enough.

Hair, my hair's not bad, it's in quite good condition, and I don't think you can tell it's dyed . . . well, not dyed, rinsed, to give it more body and light and shade they said. I tried dyeing it myself once with something called Black Magic, it looked like I'd got a melted LP on my head. It was awful, I had to wear a scarf for weeks and my hands looked like I'd been auditioning for the Black & White Minstrels. But I wouldn't say my hair was my best point.

Hands – yuk, no, not them, when I've got PMT, DMT or AMT they go all podgy and bloated – like uncooked chipolatas.

Nails – my nails aren't too bad, if they get too long they can look a bit organically grown – all sort of misshapen and curled, but I suppose they could just scrape by as a good point.

Lips, um, well, lips, the bottom one is alright, quite full and wide, but the top one is far too thin. Actually they don't look like they belong together, my top and bottom lips. Maybe the top one was grafted on at birth, maybe I was born without a top lip at all and they improvised one out of rolled flesh taken from my armpit or something. No, I'd know, wouldn't I? I doubt very much that Mum would have missed the opportunity to tell me about the hours of suffering she went through when first presented with her baby daughter sans top lip.

What about breasts? They look almost presentable when I'm lying down – I wish they could look like that all the time. They'd have to do some ground-breaking stuff defying the laws of gravity, though. I don't know how it is that some large breasts stay up. Are they empty? I'll never forget the shame of failing the 'pencil test' at school. Some perfectly formed girl read in a magazine that the way to see if you needed to wear a bra was to place a pencil under your tits and if it stayed there, then you did, and if it fell away, then you didn't. We were only fourteen, so naturally the pencil floated away from the chests of most of the class but in my case not only did the pencil stay put, but I could have got my satchel and pencil case under there too.

Belly button – that's alright I guess, nothing to write home about, though.

God, it's a bit depressing writing a list of my good points, I'd probably feel better writing a list of my bad ones, they're bound to be better than my good points.

17 April

I'd completely forgotten that Downstairs Man is coming to dinner the day after tomorrow! Realised I'd better invite some other people, I don't want to be sitting here alone with him and the Foghorn, going through topics like fitness regimes and frequency of sex in long-term relationships. Rang Sally, she wasn't in, got Lovely Dan who said they could come – thank God. Told Dan they had to get here at 5.30 – 6 p.m. latest so that I could go through suitable outfits. Dan asked if he could be excused from the what-to-wear-duty this time. For the millionth time I had to explain to him that his presence is actually more vital than Sally's because although he's a bloke, he's only technically a bloke when giving me advice about clothes and PNBs (hah!) because he's my best friend's boyfriend.

He said he didn't know what I meant about 'only technically being a bloke', so I tried to explain further – '. . . you know, sort of like a eunuch in a harem, I get all the benefits of a man's opinion without caring about what he *really* thinks about me.' He didn't say much after that and just said they'd see me on Saturday. I hope he doesn't think I think he's a real eunuch, he probably knows that I know he had that scare with some bump on one of his testicles a couple of years ago – it turned out to be a spot, but Sally says he still can't see the funny side. Now, I've got to find one other person to invite, six people is OK, isn't it? I guess I'll have to take the plunge and invite Andy – my excuse could be that he'd paid for lunch in that French place. I'll make it clear that's why I'm inviting him, so that he doesn't think I still like him. I'm aware that eight is the official correct number for a successful person's dinner party, but I don't want it to be three couples, me and Andy – it'd look too nudge-nudge, wink-wink.

NB: Must tell Sally to limit discussion of her wedding plans at dinner – Andy might think I've put her up to it and come over all faint and panicky.

18 April

Andy said yes, he'd love to come to dinner – just like that, no excuses, no hesitation ... weird ...

Did a trial run tonight, spent the whole evening rehearsing tomorrow's meal. I'd decided to do the entire thing from those 'simply take ...' recipes from the TV ads where a load of has-beens do very simple dishes but make them look posh and difficult. I prepared everything in miniature to make sure it was going to be OK and that there wouldn't be any horrible tastes or colour clashes. A bit worrying, it all seemed fine – hope it doesn't mean I've got something wrong.

19 April

Woke up in such a flap about tonight, I didn't realise how early it was and found myself at Sainsbury's, gripping the trolley, knuckles white with tension, my nose pressed up against the automatic doors half an hour before it opened. Did some shopping for Old Mrs M. as well. I didn't like the look the checkout boy gave me when he was bleeping the half-loaf and individual lonely-persons portions – he probably thought they were for me, even though I made a point of mentioning that I did an old lady's shopping for her. But I made sure they all went into a separate bag and made a great display of keeping her receipt, so he'd know I was really telling the truth. After I'd done the cooking, I laid the table, that took ages, had to redo it about 74 times, just never looked right.

Couldn't decide whether to have flowers on the table and then move them when people sat down, or have them on the counter, it's so hard to know what's right. Had a bath and decided not to shave my legs this time: a) no point, b) who cares?

About teatime sat down with nothing left to do but some major panicking.

Sally and Lovely Dan arrived about 7 p.m. – very annoying. Dan said, 'I think you look great in that' – I assume he thought he was being amusing as I was wearing my dressing gown. He immediately sat down in front of *Blind Date*, while Sally and I went through outfits. Took this opportunity to point out to him that it is most unlikely that the harems allow their eunuchs unsupervised use of the remote control. Sally picked the red silk shirt to go over my long black skirt – quite rightly pointing out that the chosen ensemble needed to be good for rushing about in, carrying stuff from the table to the kitchen, etc. The shirt was a particularly good choice because it's really roomy and I didn't want to spend the whole evening worrying about whether my bum was completely covered or not. Just as eight o'clock was approaching I suddenly realised if Downstairs Man and Foghorn arrived next, then everybody would be here when Andy arrived and that would be awful and he might think we had some chummy club. I made Sally and Dan go out and stand on the other side of the street until I gave them a signal – flicking the loo light on and off a couple of times, to let them know the coast was clear, i.e. that everyone else had arrived.

The dinner went alright, I think, no one seemed to notice that everything had been created by a supermarket rather than me. There was an awful moment when someone, I think it was Foghorn, started a conversation about what kind of sad losers put in or answer lonely hearts – I nearly fell off my chair. Everyone was agreeing with her and I was waiting for the moment when all my guests would turn to me and say, 'You rather neatly fit the profile of a lonely heart, don't you think, Jackie?' I sat there waiting for the guillotine to fall when Andy said that he could easily understand how someone who didn't know many people could think it was a good way to meet someone! Yuk, I hope he's not talking from experience – I could never fancy someone who was that pathetic. I know I considered it, but that's me, that's different, I wouldn't want to be near a bloke who'd done it.

Everyone left. Decided to clear up tomorrow, it'll give me something to do.

20 April, 5.30 a.m.

I can write this now, he's finally gone to sleep. You'll never believe it – Andy came back about an hour after everyone had gone, pressed the bell and, before I'd let him in, he said he had to know where he stood with me! He said he needed to know if I was playing him off against Carlo (it didn't seem the moment to tell him that Carlo is gay). He was saying all this from the street into the intercom, I didn't know what to do because I was wearing my dressing gown – and although it occurred to me that Andy must be a bit keen, I thought he might change his mind once he got an eyeful of me in my old dressing gown (towelling is not a very slimming fabric). I realised I didn't really have time to put together a suitable casual oh-you've-just-caught-me-clearing-up outfit, so I decided to keep most of the lights off.

After I'd let him in, he bounded up the stairs and kissed me! Attractive New Andy kissed me – ancient towelling dressing gown and all. Mercifully, I'd just brushed my teeth and thanks to his passion, it appears that I got away with the dressing gown. I couldn't really relax, though, because the vision of his hands caressing my body and screeching to an untimely halt as he came across the dense forest that was growing by the minute on my legs kept haunting me. Amazingly, Andy didn't seem to notice. Before I'd had time to work up a sweat about the absence of arousing underwear we were having torrid sex on the living-room floor. Always the way, isn't it? You spend masses of money on sexy bras and pants and end up having the first sexual encounter with the man of your dreams when you've got a candlewick dressing gown and your old school knickers on.

It was all fairly quick and passionate, so I didn't have to worry about going on top or anything unbecoming like that. Anyway, I managed to keep the dressing gown done up most of the time, so that Andy wouldn't get a glimpse of anything that'd put him off. He's obviously spending the night, so it looks like he can't have noted my failure to depilate. Got up to write this and shave my legs, in case he wakes up before me.

NB: I suppose this means he's not gay but I'd better look out for signs of bisexuality, just to be on the safe side.

21 April

Spent the rest of Sunday with Andy. Had sex again, I stayed

flat on my back throughout, holding my stomach in. I can't contemplate any other positions until I've lost some weight. If he got a glimpse of anything hanging down, folding over, or flopping on to the mattress there's no telling how he'd react. Best not to give him a fright. He obviously still hasn't realised how fat and unattractive I am. He didn't seem to want to leave straight afterwards, in fact he helped me clear up. He was unusually good at washing up – I wonder if that's an indication of bisexuality.

We went for a walk and he held my hand – eeeeek! All this affection, it's very strange. Perfect Peter's idea of affection was to wrestle me to the ground in a half nelson.

Andy brought up the subject of how we should behave at work. He said he'd like to carry on seeing me but thought it would be a good idea to be discreet at work. HELP! This is all a bit rushed, I knew where I was when I was pining for him and now all of a sudden I'm knee-deep in an adult discussion about how we're going to manage a ... a ... oh my God ... GROWN-UP RELATIONSHIP. And what's worse, with someone who actually wants to be with me – WAAAAAHHHHHH!!!! This is *not* my terrority. This is not my field of expertise. The areas in which I excel are:

1. Fancying people who don't know I exist.
2. Yearning after people who've moved thousands of miles across the planet.
3. Sleeping with people in a drunken stupor and wondering if they'll call me afterwards.
4. Sleeping with people I don't like in a drunken stupor just to make them like me and then wondering why they don't like me.

I have no experience in the 'you like me and I like you, so let's develop a mature relationship based on mutual respect and interest' area.

I am not in that learning stream yet, I haven't done the training, I don't have the right equipment, I don't even have the right shoes, I haven't sat the exams ... or even the mocks.

Andy seemed to know his way around the grown-up relationship maze, so I just agreed to the being discreet at work thing.

NB: Keep an eye out for Andy wanting to keep a low profile at work because a) he's embarrassed about being with me or b) he fancies someone else at work and doesn't want them to be put off because he's seeing me. Just thought of a very possible c) – he *is* bisexual and doesn't want Carlo to go off him.

22 April

Didn't go to the therapy session today. Sort of felt like the urge had gone now that I'd bagged Andy ... maybe I'm being over-confident – I'll go next week with a brilliant excuse.

23 April

My period must be about to start – caught myself with my head down the lavatory at 6.30 this morning, scrubbing away at that blue inkspot that's been down there for years.

The menstrual cleaning mania – it's a blessing to every woman, HAH!

27 April

One good thing about this being discreet lark is it means Andy won't be going for any groping in the photocopying room or anything like that, so there's no danger of him discovering the rolls of flesh that form when I stand up. So far, I've managed to make sure he's only touched me when I'm lying down – I'm going to keep it that way for as long as I can.

29 April

Really didn't want to go to therapy today – so I went and said nothing. I felt a bit childish but she didn't say anything either so it wasn't all my fault.

30 April

Started doing sit-ups at the gym, the only thing they seem to be giving me is steel girders for neck muscles. Perhaps I'm putting the strain in the wrong place.

NB: Efficacy of sit-ups is probably negated when followed by swift consumption of two avocado and bacon sandwiches.

1 May

Went to the cinema with Andy last night. He didn't hold my hand during the film, I didn't know whether I should hold his or not. In the end I decided it was safest not to because what if he'd turned out to be one of those people who have very specific events for holding hands and really hate you if you get it wrong. Maybe Andy is a holding-hands-while-walking type of person but a how-infuriating-that-you-tried-to-hold-my-hand-when-I'm-watching-a-film type. You never know, so I just left it.

All in all we had a very nice evening together apart from one awful, awful moment. Andy came back here (I'd shaved my legs after he'd asked me to go the movies, I knew it was a good idea to keep a razor at work). Before long we were in bed, and we were kissing away when it became clear that he was going to try and have sex with me from behind! When I first realised what he had in mind I decided not to face the oncoming danger and stayed firmly on my back, pressing my shoulders into the mattress with all my might. But he continued on this line, kind of edging his way to get behind me. I was petrified – if he saw my bum from that angle, it would all be over, game up, *rien ne va plus*. Under no circumstances was he going to get a bird's-eye view of my bottom. No matter how keen he is on me, knelt on all fours is not a flattering position for me and I don't intend to adopt it unless I'm in a coma. I needed a good excuse or else I was in big (hah!) trouble – so I told Andy I had acute vertigo. He seemed a bit perplexed at this news and then said, 'Isn't that when someone's afraid of heights?' 'Yes,' I explained, 'but I can't raise my back above sheet level.' Andy kind of lost interest in sex after that, actually I wouldn't have minded a shag but better to go without sex than lose a PNB, just because of a moment's abandon.

NB: Be vigilant at all times, there are a limited amount of complaints that are feasible excuses for refusing sex in unflattering positions.

6 May

You'll never believe it! I've been given the boot! I have been ditched! Fat Therapist has dumped me! The bloody therapist has chucked me! I went along for my session today, as usual, admittedly, I was a bit late, but I'd thought that'd give us something to talk about. Anyway, I sat there, waiting for her to say something, and eventually she asked if I'd remembered that this was our last assessment session. I said, 'Yes, of course, I've remembered.' How could I forget? I'd only kept coming so that I could earn enough points to be allocated the *real* therapist. Then she said that she'd done some thinking (I hate people who say that sort of thing) and that she didn't feel I needed therapy, and that I just needed to control my inclination to focus on minor issues! Don't need therapy? Don't need therapy? I felt like jumping out of my chair, spinning round, lifting my cardigan to reveal my arse and saying, 'Look at the size of that and try telling me I don't need therapy again.' I was fit to be tied, I can't believe I've worn jeans in that woman's presence and she still doesn't think

I need therapy! Hah! I know what the problem is, being fat herself, she hasn't faced the undeniable, universal truth that you cannot be truly happy when you've got a big bum. Well, I know this, even if she doesn't, so she probably wasn't any good at her job anyway. Maybe I'd be better off at Weight Watchers, where they really understand that being fat is evil.

NB: Check out the local WW first, to ensure I won't be the fattest person there. I'll pretend I'm looking at the hall as a possible conference venue and just accidentally-on-purpose be there on the same day they hold the WW meetings.

8 May

Went out for a drink with Andy last night. He said he thought I was great and had a wonderful body. Oh God, there's something wrong with him – I knew it, I knew it, I knew it, there had to be, why else would he ever have fancied me in the first place? Why, oh why did I fall into the trap?

9 May

Got to think, got to get away, feeling panicked, my world is crashing around me. What is going on? First, Fat Therapist doesn't think I need therapy and now Andy thinks I'm lovely – I'm going to Mum's for the weekend. It'll be hell on earth, but at least I won't have to worry about being with someone who thinks I'm great.

10 May, 11.30 p.m.

At Mum's – well, this is nice. I arrived at about 12.30 p.m., sat down to a lunch of some two-day-old salad, a couple of pieces of curled-up ham and some rock-hard bread. This appetising fare was offered up to a favourite tune from Mum's repertoire, '. . . when you are 59 perhaps you'll understand why punctuality is so important. It seems very sad that you don't have enough consideration for me to stop at a phone box. Half an hour may not mean much to you but I was looking forward to seeing you and now I've been kept waiting . . .'

I refrained, rather maturely, I decided, from remarking that judging by the spread it looked more like I was two years late. If I want to know what Mum thinks of me, I just have to look at the food she offers me. When Keith is there, you can expect a lunch of hot, fresh bread, a wide range of unusual cheeses, fine meats, exotics fruits, that really expensive salad that comes in a bag ready washed and torn (Sally calls it millionaire's salad) and, what's more, lots of it. When I come here alone, I count myself lucky if I'm offered anything that's less than a month past its sell-by date.

Another favourite pastime of Mum's is to lure me in for the kill and this weekend's been no exception. This evening, she acted like there was nothing she wanted more than to sit down and share a bottle of wine with me, have a few nibbles and hear my news. So, just as I'd been lulled into a warming sense of security (false, naturally) and was telling her about the Pozzi conferences, I leant forward to take a handful of crisps and WHAM!, she pounced on me with the speed of a leopard, her voice pinched and her mouth in full hen's-arse mode – 'Have you any idea *just* how many calories there are in those? Do you know what it's like for me, having to watch you chomp your way through those nuts? Is that your third glass of wine? Has it ever dawned on you that wine is filled with sugar? Do you ever think you might have a drink problem?'

My reaction? Well, I had a range of options available to me: regress to nine years old, burst into hot, furious tears and yell incoherently; point out to her, rationally and calmly, that I am fully up to date on the calorific content of most foods currently available in Western society; or, take an even larger handful of crisps than originally intended and stuff them into my mouth, crunching them as noisily as possible. As usual, I went for my personal favourite – number three. You see, that way I still get to eat the crisps *and* really annoy my mother into the bargain. I didn't get where I am today without having worked out that my eating habits serve as a marvellous device for winding up my mother. After all, it's all her fault, she may as well pay for it.

NB: Does everyone turn into a truculent thirteen-year-old when they go home, or is it just me?

The thing about Mum is she never knows when to give up – she's like a rabid dog with a dead rat hanging between its bared fangs, wearing away at its lifeless body, froth everywhere. She was probably a hyena in a previous life. She'd obviously decided that this weekend was the optimum time to catch up on her mission to ruin my life/make me feel worthless/knock out any self-esteem I might have managed to muster since we'd last seen each other and generally bring me up to date on what a huge disappointment I'd been to her. She was on a roll and nothing was going to stop her. I finished off the bowl of crisps – I didn't really want them but I had to show her I hadn't been defeated. Mum was sitting there, her mouth now firmly sphincter-like, knitting – a deafening cacophony of clacking needles, she's very good at 'angry knitting'. So I turned the TV on, and she was off again, seizing the opportunity for a second bout of withering ... 'oh, this mindless rubbish, is this the sort of entertainment that you and your friends find amusing? Don't you ever read a book? I only have it for the news and those marvellous wildlife programmes. Are you so empty-headed that some cretin sitting behind a desk blabbering meaningless nonsense away to other cretins serves as a diversion for you?' I toyed with the idea of telling her that my absolute favourite programme of all time was *Beadle's About*, then decided I couldn't be bothered, the genius of my riposte might be lost on Mum, as I couldn't be sure she'd know who Jeremy Beadle was.

Gosh, I am glad I came up here, just think, I could have been having a weekend with a nice, attractive man who thinks I'm fabulous – but I didn't fall into that trap, not me, oh no. I'm ahead of Andy, the more time he spends with me, the less he's going to think I'm great. It stands to reason, the more he sees me, the more chance he's got to discover things he doesn't like and go off me. In a way, I should be grateful for this refresher course with Mum, it keeps me on my toes, keeps me alert to the pitfalls of self-confidence.

11 May

Woke up feeling really stiff this morning, hardly surprising as

I'd gone to bed rigid with tension. I'll bet Keith sleeps like a newborn baby when he's up here – *natch*. Made the error of taking Mum out to lunch before I left, foolishly forgetting that would involve a drive, with me at the wheel. Even though I am extremely careful to keep well below ten miles an hour whenever Mum is in the car, she invariably behaves as if she has been forcibly strapped into the front seat of a runaway helter-skelter. She's sucking her teeth, doing sharp intakes of breath, squeezing her eyes tight shut, frantically grasping at her seat belt if another car appears three miles away on the horizon, usually screeching something like, 'Have you any idea how close you are to that car? You're completely out of control, is this what passes for normal driving in London?' Once again, I exercised enormous restraint and didn't go into a wheel spin while leaning over, opening the passenger door and pushing her out – tremendous maturity on my part, I feel. Found myself flooring it on the way back to London. Excessive speed isn't really going to pay Mum back for annoying me so much, though. Maiming myself in a car crash would probably be worse for me than for her but, on the other hand, if I died instantly it would definitely be worse for her, so you never know.

14 May

I can't believe it, I'm dumbstruck. When I got home from the weekend there was a message from Perfect Peter on the answermachine. Apparently he's going to be in London for a few days soon and would like to see me – GOSH! I've kept the message on the tape, Sally's coming round at the end of the week and we can go over it with me then, maybe she'll be able to shed some light on what he means.

18 May

Mr Bowyer's secretary came round at work today with a memo about a Management Away Weekend he's organised for some of the senior managers in October – eeeeek! Apparently it's going to be held at some luxury hotel in the country, with guess what – an indoor pool! What marvellous news, how I relish the opportunity to appear in a swimsuit in front of a selection of my colleagues. I guess I'll have to organise a plaster cast for myself, or say I've got something catching like leprosy ... mmm, that might not be such a brilliant idea ... an ear infection might be slightly less unappealing.

Andy asked if he could pop over this evening. I really wanted him to but said no. Sally's coming round to help decode Perfect Peter's message and I don't want to put her off. Anyway, Andy might have been testing me to see if I'd say yes and then once I did, he'd think, 'Oh, that's a bit pathetic, whenever I ask her if I can pop over, she always says yes. Doesn't she have a life?', so it's probably quite good that I wasn't available.

19 May

'Hello, there, Jackie, long time no see. I'm still slaving away trying to make my first million here in the Big Apple. I've got to be in London soon, so I thought I'd give you a tinkle, eh, eh, and see if you fancy getting together, shoot the breeze, go over old times, hear my news, swap news, generally have a bit of a face-to-face. Over and out for now, I'll ring when I touch down in old Blighty.'

'What kind of a twat speaks like that?' was Sally's first, helpful remark, upon hearing the above. (I thought it'd be easier if I wrote it down verbatim, so that I can erase the tape.) 'Good God, I thought he was a plonker when you were going out with him, but this just confirms it even more. I can't believe you are seriously considering meeting up with him.' Sally was in a bit of a bate. She started going on and on ... 'now, you've got someone really nice, who accepts you exactly the way you are, unlike so-called Perfect Peter, whose idea of a lovely birthday gift for you was a bumper pack of Slim Fast!' I was a bit annoyed because Sally was focusing on the meaning of the message itself rather than each individual word ... I wanted to know, for example, what she thought he meant by '... hear my news, swap news ...' I persisted with my desire for a word-by-word breakdown but Sally wasn't having it ... 'I don't know, maybe he's got no news, it's just an excuse, maybe he fancies a quick leg-over when he's in London and you're probably the only woman left with a pulse who'll have anything to do with him. Do I have to remind you that this man played you like a giddy kipper before he jetted off to New York without so much as a by-your-leave?' Mmm, I was rather hoping that Sally wouldn't feel she had to remind me of that actually, but, still, I was glad to hear that she thought he might still have feelings for me.

21 May

Saw Andy yesterday night, he'd rung up in the morning and asked if I was free – sweet. We had a nice time, but I couldn't get Perfect Peter out of my mind. Weird, isn't it – how you go out with someone who's made you feel fat and ugly the whole time you've been with them, then chucks you, leaves the country and never contacts you again, and yet you stay always feeling like they were the one?

26 May

Had a briefing this morning with Bossy Bowyer and Carlo Pozzi, it's the next conference in Birmingham in a couple of days. I must say Carlo hides his true sexuality very well, you never get a whiff of it, for a moment. He gave me the most beautiful scarf that he'd brought back from a weekend in Venice, as a thank you present for the first conference. If only straight men had such good taste.

Later on in the day, Andy came up to my desk and asked me what I thought of Carlo – I didn't know what to say. Before I could think of an answer, Andy said, 'I would imagine a lot of women find him very attractive, wouldn't you? It's hard for a bloke to tell, but he's pretty eligible, isn't he? You work with him quite closely, what do you think?' Why would Andy ask me questions like that? If this is his way of getting round to the subject of his bisexuality then it's a bit cruel – why should I be dragged into his secret life, confirming for him Carlo's immense attractiveness?

30 May

The second conference today, I wore my blue suit and that scarf Carlo gave me, which was perfect because it's quite long, so when my stomach bulges out as I sit down I could spread the scarf out carefully beforehand so it covered most of my midriff. When we were all standing about Carlo remarked on me wearing it, it was nice that he remembered having given it to me – gay men are so sensitive. The whole thing went well and everyone seemed happy – oh, except Andy. He kept stomping about, not saying much – at one point he was even quite snippy with Carlo. Is this his way of letting me know that he's started to go off me? I suppose it's about time, he's been keen on me for nearly six weeks now, and that bloody cellulite mantra floated out from under the fridge the other morning, when he was there. So although he hasn't actually seen the cellulite in the flesh, as it were, he now knows I've got it, so his loss of interest in me is only to be expected, I guess. Oh well . . .

I'd been on the verge of asking him to come to Dad's sixtieth, that was a lucky break. Just as I'd have been plucking up courage to say, 'I wonder if you'd support me at a frightening family event,' he was probably sorting through a selection of plausible excuses for not wanting to see me any more. I left Birmingham without saying goodbye to anyone, no point in hanging around waiting to be chucked.

1 June

There was a message from Jennifer on the machine when I got

back – she needs to know if I'm bringing anyone to Dad's thing – hah bloody hah, I'm not going to dignify that snide joke with a response. Rang Keith to check that he wasn't bringing a girl – highlighting my status as the family 'single one'. He said he wasn't, but that if it was going to make me feel bad, he might consider hiring one just for the occasion – hilarious.

Popped in to see Old Mrs M. this morning, I was feeling a bit guilty, hadn't seen her for a while. She was on good form, she said she'd heard a bit of to-ing and fro-ing from my flat and wanted to know what had been going on. I told her all about Andy (obviously not all, I mean I left out the bit about him trying to have sex from behind – I'm pretty confident they didn't do *that* in the old days). She was really pleased and said that Andy sounded like a 'straightforward sort of fellow'. I decided not to tempt fate and tell her that it looked like it might all be over any minute now.

4 June

God! Perfect Peter has rung and wants to meet me for a drink tonight. It's a bit short notice, and I was supposed to be doing something with Sally, but at least he said he was sorry that he hadn't rung sooner – he arrived a week ago but apparently things have been a bit hectic since. I can understand that. Didn't dare tell Sally, I said he'd rung a couple of days ago, but that I'd forgotten. Sally said, 'What about Andy?' and I told her that he'd been a bit cool with me since the last conference and that I was expecting to get some embarrassing brush-off from him any minute now. Sally was really annoying because she said she didn't believe Andy wanted to chuck me and that there must be something going on I hadn't told her about. But there isn't. If only my life was that interesting! God, if only someone else was interested in me I'd be able to be much more confident about Andy because then I'd know that he wasn't the only member of some loonies' club that finds me attractive.

10 June

Oh joy, oh rapture – I don't need you, I don't need Andy, I don't need anyone. I'm on top of the world and it feels great. My problems are all over, my life is back on track, I am IT. Yeah, yeah, I suppose you want to know what's happened. Well, here goes. I slept with Perfect Peter – oh, yes, yes, yes! The man who left me has come back – that means everything is fine now, it must be he still wants me. I'll explain. We met up for a drink, I wore that black crêpe-de-chine dress which was a very good choice, because the first thing he said when he walked into the bar (he was half an hour late but I didn't say anything) was 'I see you've dropped a bit of flesh since we were together' – I was so pleased! We had a great evening, we went out for supper but I didn't eat anything in case he thought I wasn't concerned about putting on weight. He told me all about his life in New York, his flat, what he does at weekends, in the evenings, where he goes jogging, what his car is like – gosh, I heard absolutely everything about his life over there. I began to realise that he must still like me a lot if he wanted to talk about himself for the whole evening. It fact, it turned out that we talked so much about his new life we never managed to get round to hearing any of my news, but I guess there'll be time for all that.

Anyway, we'd had a couple of bottles of wine, well, he had, and then he said, 'Listen, it'll have to be at your place because the hotel get a bit funny about me bringing people back.' I couldn't believe my luck, thank God I'd shaved my legs, thank God I'd been going to the gym, thank God I'd been in when he rang, thank God I hadn't got myself a life since he'd left me. He came back here and we had sex, it was great, he only said one thing about my body still being a bit flabby, and he is right, so really he was just being honest, but otherwise it was lovely. I can't get over how lucky I am to have Perfect Peter again, all the self-loathing, all the doubts, all the worries are out of the window. Perfect Peter wants me and I'm on top of the world.

14 June

Haven't heard from Perfect Peter since we slept together but I'm sure he's just really busy, he kept saying he had masses to do while he was in London, so I'm not surprised.

Now – Andy. I guess I've got to do something about him now that it's all on again with PP, it's only fair. He's still being a bit sulky but he hasn't said anything yet so I'll tell him it's over. That's probably what he's being sulky for anyway, that's the way blokes are when they want you to chuck them so that they don't have to do it. It's not as if he's going to mind, he's obviously gone off me, so, in a way, I'm probably doing him a big favour. This way he won't have to feel all guilty and sorry for me, which seeing as we work together is quite a good thing.

16 June

Well, I went into Andy's office and said, 'I think we should stop seeing each other' and he said, 'Oh, I guessed as much, well, I hope you'll be very happy.' What does he mean? – '... guessed as much, I hope you'll be very happy' – he's the one who made it perfectly plain he'd lost interest. Oh, it's pointless speculating over that now, because that's history and I've got Perfect Peter, so who cares what Andy meant. Oh, I can feel it, my life is going to be so great from now on – I wonder if we'll live in New York or here. I'm sure I could get a transfer to our New York office easily, or maybe PP wouldn't want me to work ... whatever makes him happy is good enough for me. I feel so alive, so brilliant, so thin!

NB: Still no word from Perfect Peter but that's to be expected. Anyway, I don't think you *have* to talk to someone every day when you know it's the real thing. I'm right in my PMT time – so I'm probably over-focusing on a non-existent problem, like you do, I'm sure PP's silence is completely meaningless.

20 June

Gosh, things have been hectic. Made the ghastly mistake

of confiding in my now ex-best friend Sally, all about my romantic reunion with PP. I've realised that Sally is really jealous of my life and isn't really my friend at all. She just wants me stuck in some sad relationship with any bloke who thinks I'm nice and not to break away from the 'ugly fat friend mould' that she has kept me stuck in all these years to make her look all beautiful and gorgeous. That's definitely it, why else would she get so angry about my wonderful news? She went completely berserk and said why couldn't I see that Peter was using me and that I'd thrown away someone really worthwhile for an arsehole! She made no sense at all. I didn't bother to try and defend myself because it was clear that all her ravings were fuelled by her envy and that she was just furious because Peter is so glamorous and successful and she could never get anyone as brilliant as him. We parted on very bad terms but I don't care, because I don't need her now, or her boring, reliable boyfriend.

25 June

Knew it, knew it – Peter's rung. He wants to see me tonight, thank God I'd cancelled all arrangements to wait in for his call. He didn't say why he hadn't rung sooner and I didn't ask, I sort of wanted to but I know he hates it when I'm all insecure and vulnerable – anyway, I'm really confident about our future together now, so I don't really need to ask, do I? He said he was too busy to see me for supper or anything and that he'd just come round here when he'd finished what he was doing but that he didn't know what time it'd be and that I'd just have to wait up until he got here. How flattering that he wants to see me even though he's so busy and the fact that he wants me to wait up for him just proves how important I am to him. I knew I was right about us – yah-boo and sucks to you, Miss Sally know-it-all.

26 June, 6 a.m.

Just woken up in a rather unappealingly crumpled pile on the sofa. I must have fallen asleep after the TV stopped transmitting – that's about 4 a.m., isn't it? Really strange, Perfect Peter hasn't turned up – I wonder what on earth can have happened to him?

8 a.m. – I've rung every hospital (NHS and private) in the Greater London area but no one by the name of Peter Noyce, or answering to his description, has been admitted, so that's a big relief. Oh God, what if he's been kidnapped?

I don't have Peter's hotel number – he said there was no point in me having it as he was hardly ever there, I wish I'd done 1471 the last time he called. Actually, it's just as well I don't have it, because he might just have got held up with a client or something and he'd be really irritated if I did ring him up and interrupted him or woke him up or disturbed him in any way.

Must stop being so insecure, it's ridiculous, there is going to be a perfectly obvious explanation for why he didn't appear last night and I mustn't give in to such pathetic worries – GROW UP! Whatever I do, I *must not* make the same mistake I did when we were going out together before – talking to him about my concerns. I distinctly remember from that *34 Steps* book about getting men to marry you that they don't like hearing all that stuff – it just annoys them. It definitely says that men react very badly to hearing about women's worries and doubts. When he rings I'll just act like nothing's happened and that it isn't a problem at all that I waited up all night for him. Goodness, it's not *that* big a deal, really! Went to the gym – did three punishing classes in a row – don't want to disappoint PP when we meet up again. He's put on quite a lot of weight since he's been in America actually, but men can sort of get away with it more, can't they? Anyway, fat men are not as repulsive as fat women, it's true, but why is that?

28 June

There was a message on the answermachine from Sally when I got in – I would quite like to talk to her actually but I'm not going to call her back. She's only going to have some silly idea about PP not phoning meaning something that it doesn't mean and I don't want to hear all that nonsense. He is going to ring, I know he is. I am a better person since he left me the first time, it's obvious, he wouldn't have wanted me again otherwise, would he?

30 June

Andy came up to me today and said he'd taken a transfer to

our Edinburgh office – oh. I wanted to talk to him but I had to race back to my desk in case Peter rang.

7 July

No word from Peter, I'm beginning to feel a bit concerned. Could Sally have been right about him being an arsehole, or did he see the residual cellulite?

9 July

I think I'm going out of my mind – I've gone over and over the evening I spent with PP minute by minute, I just can't work out what I did that put him off. He never saw me from behind – that can't be it; I hardly spoke – so that can't be it; I did everything he wanted in bed, even though it did nothing for me, so I don't think it's that. What have I done to annoy him?

11 July

There was a note from Mrs M. on my mat when I got home asking me to pop in. I felt a bit bad but I couldn't go across the hall, in case Peter rang and I didn't get to the phone in time. Maybe I should buy a cordless phone, then at least I could have a bath.

14 July

I hate myself now more than ever before. I've just seen Downstairs Man – I'm going to emigrate. Oh, the shame. I bumped into him when I went down to get the post and we were chatting away about this and that (I'd managed to edge up the stairs again, so I could hear the phone) and he casually mentions that he's going to a friend of Foghorn's wedding in New York the weekend after next. It turns out that this friend, an ex-model (as if she could be anything else), is marrying someone she's being dating for the past year and his name is ... oh God, I can hardly bear to write it down ... Peter fucking Noyce, Peter fucking bloody Noyce, Peter fucking, bloody, arsing Noyce, the one and only Perfect Peter, HAH! I thought I was going to faint, the hairs on my arms stood on end, the hall span round and as I clutched at the banister, I weakly spluttered out, 'Is he a lawyer?' – the answer was yes, as if I didn't already know.

Oh God, the disgrace, the humiliation, Sally was right of course, why, oh why didn't I listen to her? Oh help, and now Andy's transferring to Edinburgh – mind you, he'd gone off me anyway, hadn't he? So, no great loss there, but you never know, I might have been able to hang on to him for a bit longer, specially if I'd kept going to the gym. How could I have been so stupid? Perfect Peter had always made it obvious he thought I was faulty – what on earth possessed me to think that he thought of me in any other way? I should have known nothing had really changed, he's the sort of bloke who only ever drinks very good wine and, once in a blue moon, will open a bin-end bottle for fun – it appears that I was his plonk for a night.

NB: I'm definitely going to have liposuction now, I can't wait, I'll take out a bank loan.

17 July

I'm trying to keep a low profile at work – I don't want anyone to notice that I've been chucked, well, not even chucked, to be chucked you have to have been going out with someone, I've been ... sort of sampled. I feel like a sticky bun Peter was offered, which he took a sniff of, pushed around on the plate and then decided wasn't fresh or tasty enough for him. I suppose if I were a hand-baked French patisserie croissant that might just have been good enough for him! I just know I've got that look now, that air about me that lets everyone, everywhere know with one glance that I am a chucked person, a 'chuckee'. It's the absolute opposite of that look people have when they are in love. No matter how much of a gargoyle someone is, if they are in love they have that spring in their step, accompanied by that infuriating I'm-in-an-exclusive-secret-special-club-and-you-don't-know-the-password smugness. Well, I've got the other look, I can just feel it exuding out of me, the don't-look-at-me-I'm-the-twit-who-made-long-term-plans-based-on-a-five-minute-convenience-shag. Even on the bus, where they surely can't know about Peter, I hang my head and just want to fold my shoulders into my chest and disappear.

19th July

I'm only going straight into work these days and coming straight home, I can't go anywhere in case anybody gives me a sympathetic look. Coming home on the bus yesterday, a really ugly woman sat next to me, she didn't even look around for other empty seats, she just came straight up to the one next to me and sat down. She definitely gave me a 'well, we're in the same boat now' look, like she'd recognised something in me, some sort of ugly kindred spirit. A 'people nobody wants to get off with' version of the freemasons' special handshake or eyebrow-raising or whatever it is that they do. That patronising 'I know where you are coming from' look. Well, I do not wish to have an ugly person know where I am coming from. I only want thin, beautiful people to know where I am coming from, thank you very much. I'm going to ring Sally.

22nd July

Sally's had a brilliant idea. I told her all about what had happened with the LYING PIG as, yuk, I don't even want to write it down, Peter shall henceforth be known. I showed her the *34 Steps* book and she said it was all rubbish, and that now was the perfect time to write my self-help book. Sally said those books are always written by a male psychiatrist or some anorexic, rich woman who's never actually been at the coalface of fatness or low self-esteem or no charisma or whatever it is you think you haven't got or, have got but want to get rid of. She said it'd be a really good way of channelling all the murderous feelings I have towards the Lying Pig, and as an added bonus, it'll stop me pinching myself with regret over Andy, who continues to be really sweet to me! I suppose that proves he was going to chuck me, if he'd really been keen on me he'd be foul to me now, wouldn't he? That's the rule of thumb, isn't it? When a bloke likes you, he ignores you and is rude to you and if he's not that interested in you, he's pleasant and polite . . . unless, of course, he's gay, like Carlo, and then it's different.

NB: I should probably include a chapter on 'How to Get Yourself Chucked' – I seem to be a bit of an expert in that field.

MY SELF-HELP BOOK

So OK, now I'm going to write my own brilliant self-help book. I can do it in my spare time, which I now seem to have more of than I suspect I would if I were really popular. Anyway, I've been looking through some of my self-help books and not only are they really, really helpful and informative but they're dead easy to write and they give you something to read on the loo. So not only can I help other women like myself but I can probably make loads of money.

First off, I've noticed you've got to use a really big typeface, this is for two very important reasons – that way it reads like earth-shattering, hot-off-the-press information *and* best of all it fills up the page really quickly, so you hardly have to write anything. Now, here are a few of the typefaces I tried out on the computer at work . . .

OK, what about this one – Christ, talk about heavy, this one just sort of screams FAT PERSON'S WRITING, no this won't do at all.

This one? Mmmm, no, don't really like it, it looks all

tight-arsed and penny-pinching, sort of mean-spirited. Dickens would probably use this one to write Scrooge if he had a word processor and was alive, of course.

What about this one ... oh, I don't know, it looks a bit child-like, it says I'm too stupid to write joined up.

Oh, I quite like this one . . . it sort of gives the impression that I'm thinking aloud, sharing my thoughts in an intimate style – which is what those books do, don't they? They sort of share the secrets of the author's lifestyle and make the reader realise how crap their way of living has been until they read whatever book it is, then having made you feel awful it tells you how you too can have a brilliant new life like the author's got. Until you buy another self-help book, when you realise that your previous new way of life was also crap. Probably quite a good idea to write lots of self-help books under different pseudonyms so I can take advantage of all the millions of little things different people might be persuaded to think is wrong with their lives. You've only got to get someone in a bookshop on a bad day and depending what they're feeling low about they'll probably buy loads of books over the course of a year . . . well, I do anyway. Thing about this typeface is that it looks quite romantic and girly . . . that's probably a good thing, though, Barbara Cartland sells tons of books, doesn't she? Thing is hers aren't really self-help books . . . unless you're a foreign princess or in love with an Arab sheik.

Chapter 1 – DATING

THE FIRST DATE

OK, so he's asked you out. Well, it's a modern world, maybe you asked him out. Unlikely, though, because you know as well as I do, if you'd asked him out he will probably have thought ... 'A drink? Go out for a drink? What for? Oh God, please don't fancy me, oh how embarrassing she fancies me, and I was only ever nice to her because I felt sorry for her being single at her age, and now she thinks I find her attractive ... etc.'

So we've established that you're going on this first date because he asked you out. First off, there are a few possibilities you must think of before the actual date:

'He's probably married and thinks I look like an easy leg-over.'

'He doesn't actually fancy me at all and just thinks a drink is a perfectly normal social exchange between two adults.'

'How pathetic is he, if he finds me attractive?'

'He has a long-term wasting disease and thinks I'm the nursey, stay-at-home type.'

Now that you've covered why he asked you out, let's deal with the date itself. On no account voice an idea about where to go, even if he asks – DO NOT SUGGEST A VENUE. This is very important, anywhere you suggest might encourage him to think a variety of things about you. See below for the helpful table of perilous possibilities to look out for:

You Suggest:	He Thinks:
A pub	'God! she's an alcoholic.'
A restaurant	'God! she never stops thinking about food.'

| A concert | 'She's so boring she's worried she's not going to have anything to say for herself.' (NB: This applies to cinema and theatre too.) |

So let him suggest where you go on this all-important first date. And girls, remember, as he's probably never going to want to see you again, it doesn't really matter where you go anyway.

End of Chapter 1.

I'm very pleased with my first chapter, it's succinct and full of punchy to-the-point info. Wish I'd had that kind of helpful manual, full of all the stuff you should think of *before* you go on a date, when I first started dating. I had to learn it all for myself, kind of trial by error. Do I mean that? Or is it trial and error? Trial and error means you try something and make a mistake, doesn't it? So you learn that way. Well, then I definitely mean trial by error because you try something, get it wrong and feel like you're on trial and you've been found guilty. What is it they say? ... yeah, forewarned is forearmed. I'm so much more experienced now, I can be a real help to younger girls who are trying to find their way in the world – helping them understand what men are *really* thinking and how knowing that in advance will boost their confidence for the actual date and therefore the relationship.

Just had a great idea, I could suggest to the publisher that after my self-help book has been published, they could then produce little short books of just specific chapters like Dating, etc. so that women could keep them in their handbags as a quick reference guide sort of thing.

OK, now some professional advice. Here we go . . .

Chapter 2 JOB INTERVIEWS

When you go to a job interview it's very important that you remember that they've never seen you before, they've only had a written application and your CV – probably, unless you're a model or something, and if you're a model you shouldn't be reading this, because a) models are not insecure – FACT and b) erm . . . reread and absorb a). So knowing this be sure that the outfit you choose makes you look businesslike, smart and *above all* thin. If the latter is not easily achieved then either buy a corset or carry a hefty shoulder bag (purpose of which to be explained further on).

Assuming the interview has gone well . . . don't really know how you tell that . . . look, let's just assume it has gone well, your next step will naturally be planning how to get out of the room. Like me, you will obviously have that ever-so-common nagging fear that as you turn to walk out of the room and they see how big your bum is they will decide not to give you the job after all. Don't worry, girls, we all think our job prospects hinge on the size of our bum . . . now get a grip and tackle this fear sensibly and rationally . . . is someone really not going to give you a job just because you've got a big bum?

Yup, that's exactly what is going to happen. But never fear, I know the best way for dealing with that and I'm going to share my secret with you. Remember the hefty shoulder bag? Well, as you stand up to leave, while you are shaking people's hands, discreetly and gracefully wiggle your shoulders, so that the bag swings behind you and covers the expanse of your bottom. This way the only thing they will notice is the bag, not your huge arse. Remember – no one was ever not given a job because their bag was too big.

If you don't own a big bag (I personally think it's a very worthwhile investment – after all, it can be used on so many other occasions for the same purpose), then there is another option, although I must warn readers that this is not foolproof.

When the interview is over, stand up and casually draw attention to something of interest outside, a peculiarly shaped cloud, a crane, a flock of birds – anything to get the employers to look away from you. In the seconds during which their attention is diverted, dash to the door and from that position of safety (with your bottom on the other side of the door, in the corridor) say your farewells. In the event of the room having no windows, substitute the distraction outside for something of interest on the desk, a paperweight, letter opener or discarded stamp, for example.

And there you have it, two fail-safe techniques to ensure you get all jobs you apply for.

End of Chapter 2

I think Chapter 2 is very good and extremely helpful, but my worry is that it sort of announces to the world that I've got a big bum and if there is a book launch or something, everyone will spend the entire time trying to see how big my bum is. It's probably quite hard to do a whole book launch with your back to the wall ... I've just had a great idea, I'll pretend I broke my leg just prior to the launch and do the whole thing from a wheelchair! Brilliant idea ...

NB: Check wheelchair access at work, might be idea to get one for there in case I put any more weight on in the future.

Chapter 3 – SEX: THE MOST FLATTERING POSITIONS

OK, so now let's deal with the 'you' as a product – a sex product. Obviously you've been dating for a while and you're ready for sex. You've been presenting yourself as a woman your date would really want to go to bed with. You've been trying to ~~kid him, trap him, lure him~~ . . . erm persuade him into thinking going to bed with you is going to be great. *Before* you do it, be afraid, be very afraid – you don't want the first time you have sex with him to be your last. It will be, if he catches a glimpse of any area of your body that is not attractive. Remember, revolting to you is unattractive to him. So before you go to bed with him, not before, like five minutes before, I mean before, like a few days before, take a good, long look at yourself naked. I know, I know, not much of a picnic but it has to be done – remember, forewarned is forearmed.

So, standing in front of a full-length, highly polished (you don't want to miss anything) mirror, take up the various poses for sex that your man might be interested in, then look in the mirror and check what bit (or bits) of your body look disgusting. Here are some examples I have tried myself at home:

The kneeling-on-all-fours position – you will notice that your breasts hang down in a very unappealing way, not to mention your stomach. I, for one, am aware that the stretch marks on my breasts are so pronounced that if a lover ever catches sight of them, the Fortuny pleat will spring into his mind and that will be the end of my hopes for a continued ~~shag~~ relationship. Although, like most women, I would prefer to sacrifice my lover than ever ~~do it~~ ~~have sex~~ make love doggy-style again.

The 'on top' position – very perilous position indeed.

Basically, I would say that this position should be avoided at all costs, unless you are fully clothed. The necessary movements of sex will send your breasts and stomach flying all over the shop in an extremely off-putting manner. In the unlikely event of your partner not noticing, I defy any women to concentrate on the matter in hand when she looks down to see the cascading folds of free-flying blancmange.

The sideways, from behind position – now this can be a good way to hide a lot of things, particularly if you manage to draw the duvet up your body (as if in a fit of ecstasy), thereby covering most of your front.

The sideways, facing each other position – really not to be recommended at all. You'll find, having checked this in the mirror, that your breasts and stomach and probably thighs, slump into three revolting mountains on the mattress in between you and your partner.

NB: Gravity is not a girl's best friend.

The standing up position – stand with your back to the mirror, bend over and look at yourself between your legs – ugly, isn't it? Well, aren't you glad you saw it first and not him?

To sum up, my advice would be stay flat on your back, preferably with the lights off. Horizontal, everything falls backwards, including your cheeks and double chin – now that can't be bad!

End of Chapter 3.

Now, I really think my sex chapter is very good indeed. It's honest, frank and tells it like it is. I got that tone from the American self-help books, they always talk to you like you're a product, which is good because you should be thinking of how best to market yourself – like cheese or something. It gives clear, sensible advice on that most terrifying of subjects – it makes sex manageable. Maybe I should call it the guerrilla guide to intercourse ... is that gorilla guide? ... no, it is guerrilla, isn't it? Like you're a warrior or rebel. Of course, I should write another chapter called the gorilla guide to sex and that would be for when you've got PMT or taken too many hormones ...

NB: Check which hormones make you grow a beard.

28 July

Spent the whole evening with Mrs M. last night watching TV. There is very limited interest one can muster in the Rover's Return's barmaid's new hairdo and what her boyfriend's sperm count is, but I felt I had to make up for my recent absence. Didn't tell her about Andy, too embarrassing, even a woman whose last horizontal contact with a man was pre-war could tell I'd behaved like an idiot.

Had quite a difficult encounter with the bank manager today. Bloody hell, try getting a poxy loan out of a bank without telling them what it's for! He kept saying he was 'amenable to the proposal' but that he wanted to know what the loan was for. I tried saying it was for investigative work into my personal development. When he asked for further explanation, I plumped for 'crucial life-saving surgery' (not a good idea), eventually I admitted it was for cosmetic surgery but not for me, for my sister (I don't think he knows I haven't got one). I couldn't tell him it was for me, I don't want to cash a cheque to a chorus of tellers sniggering and making vacuum hose sucking sounds with their lips.

Apparently the liposuction takes a day and I can be out the

same evening, but walking is a bit difficult for a few weeks after. So I'm going for a consultation tomorrow and will probably have the op the day after. I'd already organised holiday time off work and I'll go away straight after, so that way I won't be back at work until a couple of weeks after the operation. While I'm away I'll have my hair cut or dyed, I've read that doing something like that draws attention away from your new shape and that's what people think is different about you – they don't notice you've lost six inches round each thigh, I'd die if anyone noticed that.

29 July

Bored – probably ought to write more of my self-help book but I'm a bit stuck for ideas now that I've done the sex bit. I suppose it doesn't have to be a really long book anyway, with a few photos maybe I could get away with three chapters – all spaced out cleverly, obviously.

30 July

God almighty! I cannot believe the tortures women endure in the name of beauty – especially considering what most men look like. The surgeon giving me the liposuction consultation was absolutely hideous, it looked like someone had given up halfway through turning him into the Elephant Man. The nurse was reassuringly slim and pretty, reinforcing the self-loathing and intimidation required to go through with this expensive self-mutilation process. But the doctor was so unattractive, and what's more completely unashamed about being this ugly, that I began to question what I was doing. To make matters worse, when I stripped off to expose the offending regions, he sensitively said, 'Oh, yes, your problem areas are quite widespread, aren't they?' I felt like saying, 'yeah, well, have you looked in a mirror lately, because *your* problem areas are mainly concentrated on your face!' My 'problem areas' indeed! This from a man whose only real aid in life could ever be a paper bag. I know very well what my problem areas are, thank you very much – after all, I have devoted a lifetime to familiarising myself with every fold and crease that could possibly qualify as a problem area!

For the first time in my life I began to feel a sort of defiance in place of the shame I normally experience when nude. Ugly Surgeon then proudly showed me this great bucket type of thing and said, 'We anticipate filling this with your excess fat.' Good God, you could have fed a team of carthorses out of it! I was getting more and more unsure about whether I wanted to do this. I know I'm overweight but if they managed to fill that thing with all the flesh off my thighs and bottom I'd probably crack in half next time I sat down.

The deciding factor came when I asked to see some photos of post-op thighs. Bloody hell! They looked like two pieces of steak with feet! The fantasy, as put forward by Ugly Surgeon, that these thighs now looked better was the best scam I'd ever heard of. I could just see a room full of male quacks plotting ... 'Here's the plan, guys, make women feel like shit most of their lives, then do a couple of weeks' training at any old tailor's, pop a white coat on, take a cheque for anything in excess of £1,000, stick a vacuum cleaner into their thighs and Bob's your uncle.'

I mustered up enough courage to say that I was going to have to think about it. I may have sown the seedlings for self-esteem but I still wasn't ready to let rip with a lecture on the subjugation of women, only to crumple with agreement when they replied, 'yes, but when was the last time you wore a thong with confidence?' Instead I just backed out of there, hoping that they wouldn't talk about me after I'd gone.

1 August

Don't really feel like going on holiday, seems a bit pointless now that I don't have to go into hiding with bruised thighs. No one's around in the office, though, so I might as well. Andy has apparently gone to have a few days up at the Edinburgh office before he joins them after the summer. Bit of a relief, imagine if he found out I was going on holiday on my own! I'm actually not that bothered about going on my own, particularly as I won't have to worry about the whole avoiding-friends-seeing-you-in-a-swimming-costume thing. But I imagine it would just reinforce Andy's relief that he'd already gone off me.

4 August

Portugal, sunny Portugal. Just arrived at Dad and Jennifer's hacienda, it's a kidney-shaped bungalow type of thing, wrapped around a pool – yuk, it looks like something out of that failed soap opera, *Eldorado*. They are as pleased as punch with it. Don't think I'm going to be able to manage a whole ten days here, I think I'll invent some interesting friends that I have to go off and visit for a few days. Travelling on your own – that's meant to be quite good for you, isn't it? I don't mind being on my own, it's the eating alone in restaurants I can't stand. Do you read a book and look like a swot? Not read a book, then look like you're waiting for someone to talk to you? Look down at your plate all the time? In which case, you look like someone who's obsessed with food. Actually, the waiters are worse than the other customers, they either pay you loads of attention because they pity you, which picks you out, in bold relief, as 'the sad customer' or they pay you no attention at all, presumably because they think you're too tragic to bother with. If I go off on my own, I'll just make sandwiches, I'm not running the gauntlet with Portuguese waiters.

5 AUGUST

Bored, bored, bored.

6 AUGUST

Bored, hot, bored, very hot.

7 AUGUST

Had enough of this, it's boiling hot and I can only use the pool when Dad's playing golf and Jennifer's not in – not making the mistake of appearing in a bikini in front of those two again. The last time Dad saw me in one, he started a conversation about the body's difficulty in breaking down carbohydrates and then denied he was deliberately trying to make me feel uncomfortable. I've told them that I've made an arrangement to meet some friends in Lisbon, God knows where I'm really going to go but I'll be setting off tomorrow come hell or high water.

10 AUGUST

I've spent the last two days in some god-forsaken town called Escerbo – it's fantastic, there's not a human being under 90, myopia seems to have run riot in the town, so I don't think anyone's noticed I'm here *and* the beach's deserted. There is an old lady who owns the pension I'm staying in but she spends her every waking moment crouched over the TV watching topless women reading out lottery numbers – so until I come down to the reception desk in a spangly G-string with tassles on my nipples I don't think she'll be bothering about me. Still sticking to sandwiches, though, I don't want to push my luck and go to a restaurant.

Quite a palaver getting here but it's obviously paid off. Had to take a bus heading for Lisbon, in case Jennifer, who took me to the bus station, checked the destination of my bus with the depot after I'd left and discovered that I wasn't going to Lisbon after all and then knew I didn't really have friends to meet there. Once I was sure Jennifer wasn't following the bus,

I got my map out and picked the smallest town by the sea I could find that was far enough away from Dad's. I had to pick a seaside town because although I don't really like sunbathing, I've got to go back to London with a tan so that people at work know I've really been on holiday and think I've got an action-packed life ... well, just a life actually.

NB: Be careful about depth of tan. Dad and Jennifer might notice and they probably know that there aren't any beaches in Lisbon.

12 AUGUST

Got to go back to Dad's tomorrow, I'll fake a dicky tummy so that'll cover why I'm not having a wonderful time larking around in the pool. An Australian backpacker turned up this morning and asked me to show him the beach. I double-checked he actually lived in Australia and wasn't planning on coming to England before I agreed. I was careful, obviously I can't stop the *entire* world seeing me in a swimsuit but I can make sure those that do will never again be on the same continent as me.

13 AUGUST

Back at Dad's after a hideous bus journey, the whole female

population of Portugal seemed to be going my way and each one of them accompanied by a sheep!

14/15 AUGUST

Return flight from Oporto, 5.30 a.m. The flight is delayed, I'm sort of trying to sleep, slumped like a bag lady in a heap on a plastic chair which is welded on to a line of about 130 other identical plastic chairs. I wouldn't mind a drink but I can't move because my thighs are now glued to the plastic by the sweat I've produced. If I stand up I'll bet all 130 chairs will come up with me, as their central linchpin is now stuck to my arse. Even if the line of chairs doesn't come up with me I just know the sound of my sweaty flesh parting company with the hardened plastic will make that awful squelchy, sucky sound, announcing to the whole airport (which is now jammed) that I'm not just fat but sweaty too.

I bet bucket airline people deliberately schedule these flights to be this early because no one looks good at this time in the morning. That way they can bank on your confidence being really low because of how shitty you look, so naturally it follows that you daren't call attention to yourself by making a fuss if the plane is delayed for five years. We'll all just sit here meekly until some substitute plane is brought from somewhere close by, like Arkansas, rather than approach a perfectly manicured, perfectly maquillaged, perfectly slim air hostess with a pathetic query about when you might be able to plan a home visit.

9.30 p.m. The plane is finally about to take off. Haven't

eaten all day ... I wonder if I lost any weight, pity they don't have scales in the lavvies. Damn, if I'd thought of it I could have quickly popped on to the baggage weighing scales at check-in ... mind you, I think only the check-in girl can see the screen and she might have announced my weight on the Tannoy. God, that reminds me of one the most frightening flights I ever took, it nearly put me off flying for ever. I had to organise a conference in the south of Ireland and the only way to get there was on one of those tiny little propeller planes. I thought I was going to die – as you queued up to get on the plane, it turned out you had to be weighed before you got on. Thankfully they asked you to get on the scales carrying your luggage, so I loudly mentioned that I was in the building trade and was taking over some interesting new brick samples and a couple of pioneering types of lead piping in my suitcase.

My seat's really uncomfortable, I'm absolutely sure my hips and thighs weren't pressing against the arm-rests on the way out here. So I obviously haven't lost any weight, might as well have had that chorizo after all. And I'm in the middle seat – great, so I've got two witnesses to the extra weight I've evidently gained on holiday. There's some bloke on my left reading his newspaper, pretending he hasn't noticed that I'll probably need to be mechanically winched out of my seat, and on the other side there's some old Spanish lady who's looking out of the window, muttering something under her breath. She could be saying anything – wish I knew what the Spanish was for fat and greedy.

Flight landed late, something to do with extra haulage, combined with wind resistance, causing the plane to drag. The Tannoy was all crackly and distorted but I'm pretty sure the captain was saying, 'We are about to land at Gatwick Airport, ladies and gentlemen, and please let me take this opportunity to apologise for the slight delay in our arrival time. This is due to the considerable gorging a certain woman whose initials are JMP, she knows who she is, did on holiday, resulting in a hefty weight gain around her thighs and bum. Not just adding to the weight of the plane but meaning that she's probably had quite an unpleasant flight, as her thighs will have been slowly embedding themselves into the arm-rests of her seat throughout the journey. Serves her right, really, only I hope it hasn't made for too ghastly a journey for her neighbouring passengers.' Then he said something in pidgin Portuguese, probably the same again.

An interminable wait at the luggage carousel. My bag was actually one of the first off the plane but I had to wait until everybody else had picked up theirs so that nobody would see that the crappy old one was mine. It was definitely the tattiest, I wish I'd bought an expensive suitcase, I'm so embarrassed now. It's just occurred to me that this is probably exactly the sort of bag smugglers use to make them look like sad people who couldn't smuggle sand on to a beach.

Am I the only person in the world who feels guilty walking through Nothing to Declare? Do I look ahead of me resolutely and ignore the customs officer? . . . no, that'll look as if I don't like them and they might haul me up for insulting them. Do I saunter through casually taking in the customs officers and the pleasant surroundings? No, then they'll think I'm so used to going abroad that I must be a drugs courier. I know, I'll look down and sort of fix my gaze on my luggage trolley, yeah, and look a bit upset like my Portuguese boyfriend has just chucked me and they won't want to get into questioning someone who might start crying. Mmmmm, I think that's probably best, but what if they think I'm looking at the trolley to make sure my gold bullion, or drugs, or 700 cigarettes don't fall out? Oh God, what do I do? I haven't actually got anything to declare or hide but if they do question me I just know I'll feel guilty about something – anything. Knowing me I'll probably confess to the Brinks Mat robbery just for the sense of relief.

Waiting for the Tube now, went through customs and although I did break into an unattractive sweaty panic I still managed to glance at the old man whose bag they *were* looking at and give a look that suggested 'Yes, officer, that is exactly the sort of person I would also choose as likely to be up to no good.' It was a kind of interested look, which also implied that I thought the officer was clearly very good at his job for being able to see malevolence in someone so innocent-looking.

16 August

Home again, oh joy, oh rapture. Not enough mail for my liking, most of it junk anyway – still, it means there's something to open. One of them's from the Samaritans – I wonder where they got the idea to write to me . . . I don't like that at all. The letter is asking for donations but it does seem to be directed at me personally.

17 August

Filled up most of today with washing holiday clothes, ironing and disposing of items in fridge that had grown cultures. Don't know what to do now, I'm officially on holiday until the 23rd.

I can't go back into work early, that'd just make me look *too* pathetic and empty life-ish. Old Mrs M. is having a few days with her second cousin somewhere that ancient people all live. Sally and Dan are away on holiday together, of course. I've only got a few things left to watch that I taped while I was away, and I've already been spreading them out so as to have something to do in the evenings.

19 August

I've got all that special type of depression you feel when you come back from holiday. Why does anyone ever go on holiday? I feel like a holiday to get over going on holiday. Old Mrs M's back, popped in to see her, she's fine, as ever – told me that the barmaid in *Coronation Street* is pregnant so her boyfriend's sperm count can't have been as low as all that. I'm only really interested in Ross and Rachel's relationship but I don't think Mrs M. watches *Friends*. I dare say I shouldn't watch it either, it makes me laugh while it's on, but as soon as it's over I wonder why I don't have five impossibly gorgeous friends who come round my house, lounge around on my expensive sofas and laugh at everything I say. Last time I'd seen it I worked out that I was probably six times the body weight of all the girls in that show put together. And how do they do that thing with their hair, the whole mane springing and bouncing out of their scalps? The only way I can get my hair to remotely resemble Rachel's is if I blow-dry it while I'm hanging upside down. And holding a hairdryer suspended by your ankles from the door frame is not that easy. Rachel probably has her own personal hairdresser. When I attempted that style, it didn't work at all – I looked like I'd been electrocuted.

20 August

I know it probably means I'm really pathetic and sad but I started looking through *Time Out* and was reading the lonely heart ads and you know, some of them aren't too bad. Anyway, I've had it with being single, I've blown it with Andy and I'm going to do something about it – I'm going to take positive action. I'm going to make a concerted effort to make new friends. First off, I'm going to start smiling back at those people who smile at you on the Tube – I mean, they can't *all* be loonies. Also, I'm going to answer one of these ads. I think the best thing is to pick a whole bunch at random and then select a variety of people you like the look of . . . or rather the sound of . . . or is it read of – no, that's not English, is it? This is the page I picked from; it's in the lap of the gods because I didn't really want a copy of *Time Out* so I just took an old one from outside the newsagents – when he wasn't looking, though.

I'm not sure about this one, I probably wouldn't have to

worry about my weight but he does seem a bit eclectic in his tastes ... oh God, and he's put well-built *and* buxom, he must like huge women, no he won't do. Mind you, he might think I was thin and anyone who thought that is worth, at the very least, a meeting. Gosh, wouldn't it be great if he wasn't interested in me because I was too thin ... or even better went out with me and then chucked me because I was too skinny – what heaven.

● **UXB, CAN YOU LIGHT THE FUSE?** Likes anything sporty, got great energy for life. You are wild, passionate and like all outdoor and indoor activities. PO Box 1698.

What does UXB mean? Does he like *The X Files* or something? Maybe it's one of those sci-fi codes that only those people understand ... oh, that would be a disaster. Right from the off, I would be outside his 'special club' and look like some loser who didn't understand the things he and his friends probably all say to each other in the pub, when they go up to the bar to a get drink, like ... 'to boldly go' ... or 'but that's illogical, Captain'. No, forget it, I'm not writing to him, I can already feel him and his friends all ganging up on me ... I won't fit in. Imagine the shame of being dumped by a person who'd thought wearing plastic imitation Mr Spock ears was an amusing way of breaking the ice when he first met your mother. Yeah, and knowing Mum, the more I wasn't sure about him, the more she'd think he was great – definitely not writing to him.

● **MALE REPROBATE** seeks female counterpart for laughs and bad behaviour. You won't be disappointed. PO Box 4932.

Won't be disappointed? Won't be disappointed? This man has clearly failed to grasp *just* how much can disappoint me. However, he sounds like he might be fun at least. What does he mean when he says 'bad behaviour,' though? ... Obviously I know he means something to do with sex but is he talking about some weird kind of sex or did he just go to public school and uses silly euphemisms when referring to it. That reminds me of that Martin Hardy from the Brighton Conference Centre who's always going on about 'the beast with two backs' ... took me ages to work out what he meant. It sort of gives Martin away as a bit conventional apart from anything else. Oh, my word, what if Martin put this ad in ... I'd die. Can you imagine? If we arranged to meet and it was him, I'd have to pretend I was in there for another reason and leave. He'd be bound to click, though, wouldn't he? Then he'd ring his mate Philip that used to work at Pellet's and tell him that I was such a loser I'd answered his lonely heart ad.

Wait a minute, that wouldn't make him look very brilliant, would it, because he would have to admit he'd placed the ad in the first place. Glad I thought of that, I'm probably safe, then.

I've just looked over the ragbag of PNBs on offer ... doesn't look like there are any really – too many built-in dangers of being detected as 'needy and desperate' with all of them. I know, maybe I'll reconsider therapy instead ... or liposuction ... I wonder which ends up being more expensive, in the long term, pound per pound. Anyway, can't actually write to any of them because there's a huge box at the top of the page with a sort of health warning from the magazine in it – it says that they strongly advise you to tell someone that you're going to meet a stranger from an ad the first time. Yeah, right, I'm really going to do that, aren't I?!

Alternatively, I could just have 'Sad Old Bag' tattooed on my forehead.

23 August

Back at work, thank God, that's the end of non-stop hoovering, relining shelves with greaseproof paper and cutting out and sorting into product piles 15p-off coupons out of old mags – at least until next bank-holiday.

25 August

No one's really around at work, obviously people with interesting lives don't come back until the end of August. Hope my tan doesn't fade before everyone's back, otherwise all the effort I put into getting it will have been a complete waste of time.

27 August

Andy's back from his break, don't know where he went, daren't ask in case he tells me he's just returned from the holiday of a lifetime with the girl of his dreams, produces photographs of some pneumatic babe on a tropical beach followed by a 'bet you're sorry now' look. He does look great, though. Bossy Bowyer has organised a leaving party for him on 1 September. Hope Andy doesn't bring Elle Macpherson.

NB: Should I wear the dress I wore for our first date to his leaving party, reminding Andy of how it once was, or will it just remind him of my unseemly behaviour and make him realise how lucky he is to have got away? Bit risky, better not to tempt fate.

28 August

New Secretary Sarah has just come back from her holidays ... her tan looks suspiciously similar in hue to Andy's. And there's another fishy thing – they came back to work a day apart! Now that is exactly what they'd do if they were having an affair and were trying to cover it up. Has their new-found love been staring me in the face all this time and I haven't seen it? I'll have to find out. Now, what would be the most normal, casual, breezy way of asking her if she went on holiday with Andy? (Oh God, do I really want to know?) 'Hi, Sarah, nice tan, where did you get that ... and who were you with when you were getting it?' No, that sounds ridiculous. I've got to make it sound like it's something I've thought of on the spur of the moment, after all, I hardly ever speak to her. Since she witnessed my outburst in Andy's office, I've pretended I'm the really tough, efficient type who is never friendly to people below them in the office. I had to because she's never mentioned anything about the outburst or behaved in any way differently towards me or even given me a funny look – and what's all that about? How about, 'Hello there, Sarah, you're looking healthy, enjoy your holiday ... alone?' and then see if she says she wasn't alone and tells me of her own accord who she went with – mmm, this one's not bad but doesn't *guarantee* delivery of the required information. I could go for a more roundabout approach. 'Hey, Sarah, seen Andy's tan – where do you think you get a tan like that?' Now, that's quite good because if she looks at me like she thinks that's a really weird question (which it is) then all well and good, but if she attempts to answer it, then it means she feels guilty and that she probably did go on holiday with him.

29 August

Saw Sally for a drink this evening, apparently it rained practically non-stop in the Dordogne, and she and Dan argued all the time. Felt really guilty because when I heard what a dismal holiday they'd had, I was ecstatic. I was just so glad she didn't say, 'But the rain didn't matter because we spent all day in bed making the kind of beautiful love you do when you're in a fulfilling, long-term relationship' ... well, you don't want your face rubbed in it, do you?

Now, just need to hear that Foghorn and Downstairs Man have broken up and Thin Clare and Paul's engagement is off and I'll be laughing.

NB: Oh God, must, must curb fast-growing tendency to glory in others' bad news – if not, I will undoubtedly end up with the bitter and twisted person's trademark – a hen's arse mouth.

30 August

Bit thrown because Thin Clare and Bossy Bowyer's secretary are both back now and their tans are also remarkably similar in hue to Andy's and New Secretary Sarah's – so either they've all been on some secret holiday together that they planned behind my back or I'm reading too much into what you can tell from a tan.

2 September

Andy's leaving party yesterday. Mr Bowyer hadn't exactly pushed the boat out, more kind of nudged the dinghy along. It was in the big meeting room with some cheapish wine and various kinds of food that will go on sticks. I think Andy was a bit drunk, he came up to me towards the end and was going on and on about something that he'd realised while he was on holiday but he didn't say what. I was petrified it was going to be his love for another woman, or how laughable it was now to think we could have ever had a relationship, or the tremendous fun he was having footloose and fancy free. I decided it was a mistake to hang around for the outcome so I left. When I got into the office this morning there was a spidery scrawl from Andy with his e-mail address in Edinburgh on it and a note saying, 'Drop us a line some time, if you feel like it.' I can't be sure it was meant for me, maybe everyone in the office got one – he could just be looking for pen-pals.

Spent most of today briefing Andy's replacement, John

Weston. He is an extremely irritating person to work with – full of good ideas and enthusiasm, yuk.

4 September

Thought about e-mailing Andy today – couldn't decide which would look more casual, that, a fax or nothing at all. The *34 Steps* book says not to return men's calls or letters for over a week, if at all. That way they have to wonder what you are up to and it makes you seem exciting and mysterious (it doesn't say what to do when they find out you're not). It also says that you should never, ever initiate contact. Does the note Andy left count as a letter, do the same rules apply to something written on the back of an envelope? I wish they'd be more specific in those books, otherwise you might follow your own instincts and go and do something spontaneous, just like that, and then there's no telling what could happen. Don't really want to e-mail Andy from the office anyway, what if he responded, or worse still, what if he didn't? Anybody might access the e-mail and then what? I'm not doing anything. I've decided.

5 September

It's all very boring at work now. I really miss Andy. He was so kind and nice but at least I know where I am, being miserable and on my own. While I was going out with him I just kept waiting for the axe to fall and the hell to begin, so at least I don't have that constant worry gnawing away at me any more. Oh, yeah, Carlo has asked me to have dinner with him – a little unusual, I'd say, but I don't think anyone else knows he's gay so he probably feels more comfortable with me.

10 September

Going out to dinner with Carlo tonight. Gosh, it's a real relief getting dressed for supper with a gay man. I can wear what I like, within reason – obviously there's everybody in the restaurant to consider but I don't have to panic about him catching a glimpse of anything yukky.

11 September

My God! You are never, ever going to believe this! I don't think Carlo *is* gay after all. We met up in a very swish French restaurant in town and we chatted and had a few laughs about various types we'd come across during the conferences. Then, out of nowhere, he says, 'I'd like you to consider working for my company in Italy and also, more importantly, I'd like you to consider a position under me.' I didn't get it. 'Under you? Oh, as your assistant you mean?' He fixed me with his steely blue eyes and said, 'No, under me, or maybe sometimes, if you prefer, on top of me' – at first, I thought he was talking about a jobshare. The penny only really dropped when he leant over, took my hand and said, 'I think you are a wonderful woman and very desirable' – gosh! So that's what he meant by 'under me' – bit cheesy, I admit, but English isn't his first language, so he probably didn't mean to be quite as graphic as that. Well, well, well, 'very desirable' – where he comes from maybe, we all know about Italians and big bottoms, but to an Anglo-Saxon, not *that* desirable, as I'd recently discovered – to my eternal shame. I was very flattered, although the whole gay thing was still niggling away at me, but the real trouble is I can't get Andy out of my mind. I know he doesn't want me now but I still think about him. I pretended I didn't really know what he was talking about and after a while he gave up. Probably best I didn't reject him outright because then God would probably have punished me for having the confidence to think I was allowed to reject anybody.

NB: I don't *have* to get off with someone just because they want to get off with me – do I?

13 September

I hope Carlo doesn't tell Mr Bowyer that I wouldn't sleep with him ... maybe I should have, he is a big client after all and I don't want Bossy Bowyer thinking I'm not doing my job properly. Keen John Weston would probably have slept with him at the drop of a hat and without even being gay necessarily, just to be brilliant at his job, at all times.

15 September

Work is hectic but not very interesting. I've got to make

a comprehensive chart with every conference venue in the country, their facilities and costs. Then I've got to divide them up into categories of how they compare in terms of different criteria – price-to-size, service, accessibility, availability, etc. And do you think this was my idea? No, it was Keen John Weston's, natch. I mean it is quite a good suggestion but what's he doing with enough energy to adapt to a new job, smile and be pleasant all the time *and* focus on my work! He probably does voluntary relief work in Africa at the weekends.

Went out for a meal with Sally and Lovely Dan – felt like a gooseberry.

NB: I wonder why it's gooseberry? It's a small, round fruit, covered in little hairs – just like me, small, round and hairy . . . great.

16 September

Keen John came up to me today and we were talking about this chart thing. I managed to force out a compliment and he said that it wasn't his idea, he'd got it from some notes he'd looked through from a brainstorming meeting last year and apparently it is just an extension of some idea I had. Great, so he's not just keen, he's a saint too.

18 September

Can't think of a relaxed, off-the-cuff way to find out if anyone else in the office has heard any news of Andy. *Could* ask Bossy Bowyer . . . thing is, I don't want to hear about how he's getting on in the office, I just want to make sure he hasn't got engaged or anything like that and Bowyer isn't very likely to know that kind of thing.

19 September

I've realised I'd better spend that loan I got. I can't give it back because then the bank manager will know that it was for me and not for my 'sister's' plastic surgery at all (which he probably knew all the time anyway). He'll scorn me for not having the self-love to improve myself. It's £800 – what on earth shall I do with it? If I leave it sitting in the account, he'll notice that too.

22 September

I've just bought a flotation tank – they are great. I had to do something constructive with the money and I didn't think I could fit a Nordic walking machine into my flat so I bought the tank. Well, actually I didn't buy it, I got a time-share in one. I can go there six times a year for only £500. Five hundred divided by six is . . . £83.33 recurring. OK, so that's a *bit* more expensive than therapy but probably better value in the long run because it makes you feel all light-headed and you completely forget everything, which is much better than having to remember every bit of your past. As I had some money left over I decided to have a colonic irrigation. The place where I bought the tank time-share had a special on them and I've always really, really wanted to have my colon irrigated so I went for it. Can't say it's the most comfortable experience I've ever had but I came home feeling as light as a feather – nothing actually came out but they said over the next few weeks I'd notice a dramatic change.

24 September

Maybe the flotation tank wasn't such a great idea. I told Sal and Lovely Dan and he said he thought it was disgusting – he said you can't be sure what anyone else has done in there . . . it did make me think but I'm sure they clean them out, don't they? It is pitch dark inside, so it's true that there could easily be a piece of poo or something floating about an inch away from your face and you'd never know . . . oh, help, I don't think I'll be able to do it again.

NB: Just had a brilliant idea. I could get the salon to make up vouchers for one-off sessions in the tank and I could give them as presents (obviously not to Sal after what Dan said).

27 September

Don't think I'll do much more of that smiling back at people on the Tube any more. Smiled at some bloke today who then came up and said that there wasn't enough hugging in the world and didn't I think we should do something about it. Also it looked like he had a bunch of keys in his trouser pocket, but I don't think it was.

29 September

Still missing Andy. Ate two large bags of Kettles crips – felt sick. I wonder if getting off with Carlo would make me stop missing Andy. Course, there's no guarantee Carlo still wants to get off with me – might have been a once-only offer.

NB: Must stop moping – soon.

NB: Must find out if you can get liposuction and other fat-reducing surgery on the NHS. Oh, while I'm at it might as well find out about therapy as well (can't extend the bank loan now that I've already spent the money). Not going back to Ugly Expensive Surgeon or Fat Therapist.

NB: Wear very tight hat or beret and look extremely surprised next time I go into the bank, that way the manager will think I've had a facelift and that's what I used my loan for.

30 September

God, they weren't kidding when they said I'd notice a dramatic change over the next few weeks, but this is *not* the kind of change I had in mind. I thought I was on a one-way ticket to a colostomy bag when I went to the loo this morning. I seemed to have lost all muscular control in that area – it was supposed to make me lose weight, not the will to live. It was as if I'd been anaesthetised from the waist down – I seemed to have no muscular control whatsoever in my nether regions. Saw Cheeky Window Cleaner on my way out, he said he thought I was looking a bit peaky, I restrained from snapping back, 'yes, well, so would you if the world had just fallen out of your arse' – I don't really know him well enough to say that kind of thing.

1 October

Still feeling a bit weak but the 'fall-out' seems to have subsided a bit. At least I managed to get to the bus stop this morning without having to walk imagining I was holding a teaspoon in between my buttocks, like the salon told me to do.

3 October

It's the Management Away Weekend tomorrow – oh, what a laugh that's going to be. I'll probably end up getting blasted at the dinner/dance on Saturday night, do a striptease and then try and snog someone wholly inappropriate, like Bossy Bowyer – all resulting in my swift dispatch from the Pellet Corporation. Now that I've turned down Carlo, it's not likely that I'd be welcomed with open arms at his firm either. It might be more sensible to go teetotal for the whole weekend. I doubt whether Mr Bowyer is as tolerant as Andy – ah, Andy, wonderful Andy.

5 October

Hideous weekend. However, did manage to stay miles away from the pool the whole time, quite a feat as there seemed to be an unnatural amount of activity centred round it. For a while, I thought it might have been a conspiracy of Thin Clare's to humiliate me, she, naturally, looked very undermining, i.e. good, in her swimsuit. I must say she was very relaxed chatting and even *eating* in it – I just can't believe someone could feel so at ease in a swimming costume. Couldn't organise a plaster cast in time, and anyway I'd have had to keep wearing it back at work too, so I went for the 'ear infection' – think I got away with it. Of course, I could have just told the truth, plain and simple – 'Excuse me if I don't partake in any poolside recreation but, apart from the fact I'd rather run naked down Oxford Street than appear in front of my colleagues in a swimsuit, my bowel movements are currently not under my complete control, so I'll opt out if it's OK with everyone' – somehow I think the ear infection was a bit more savoury.

Made the mistake of taking up the offer of a cheap massage from the woman running the sauna at the hotel. The massage itself was fine but it made me go all wobbly and bendy, and I kind of lost my balance on the way back to my room – in front of Keen John Weston and Thin Clare. The last thing on earth you ever want, when you trip up anywhere, is for anyone to help you. It only makes you feel 900 times more stupid than the falling over did. I just planned on lying there quietly, sort of blending into the carpet, and then crawling along the hall towards my room when the coast was clear, desperately hoping that nobody'd noticed. No such luck. John and Clare came rushing over in a flurry of concern, lots of 'are you alright?' and 'poor you, that looked nasty'. The only thing I had to be thankful for was that my dressing gown (newly bought for the occasion) hadn't flown open in the fall.

Other than that, it was the usual thing, constant eating, constant drinking and constant talking about work to people you see all the time – at work. I don't know why people bother with these jollies, everyone only ever talks about work – it's exactly like being in the office except with a running buffet. Actually, the food was pretty good but obviously I couldn't tuck in in front of everyone – I managed to sneak a doggy bag (well, more of a holdall actually) up to my room so that wasn't too bad, I had some nice snacks in the night.

NB: Disposed of nocturnal chomping evidence in one of those plastic laundry bags and took it away with me at the end of the weekend.

7 October

Sally's asked me what I want to do on my birthday. God, I'd forgotten it was my birthday next week! Marvellous, I'll be 35, oops, I put that I was 33 at the beginning of this, didn't I? Alright, I lied. Well, I couldn't be sure I wouldn't lose this.

Anyway, I could be 290 and it wouldn't make any difference. Once you're past your sell-by date it doesn't really matter how old you are. Perhaps Mum will cheer me up by sending me another lovely present like she did last year – an old book of suicidal poems which had been in her upstairs lavatory for the last six years. When I dared to make a comparison between that and the state-of-the-art laptop computer Keith had been given for *his* birthday, her reply was 'Don't be so materialistic and limited, just because the book is old, it doesn't mean it isn't interesting, you boring, stupid girl!'

And if things really go to plan, then my dad will forget my birthday until about a week after the event and then send me a card with a vintage car on the front, or a hot-air balloon, or something else hand-picked to reflect his in-depth knowledge of my interests in life.

NB: I wonder why someone came up with those designs. Were they inundated with letters? 'Dear Card Designer, try as I might, I cannot find a birthday card with an old watermill on the front, nor one depicting a clown crying, nor one with a winsome-looking puppy emerging from an old tramp's boot. The aforementioned images reflect precisely that which I wish to convey when sending greetings to a relative. Please do something to rectify this situation immediately.'

9 October

Dragged myself to the gym on my way home from work, only because I'd seen Goldie Hawn on TV last night saying the only way to get over a failed love affair is physical exercise. Mmmm, being a rake-thin millionaire movie star I shouldn't think her experience in the 'chucked' department is *that* extensive. Only managed three sit-ups – who cares?

Went back to the salon to ask about the gift vouchers for the flotation tank and got talked into booking a facial peel for the day after tomorrow. Do I really want my face skinned two days before my birthday? Question is, do I really want my face peeled at all? Well, it might cheer me up.

11 October

OW, OW, OW! Now I know how a rabbit feels. I can't believe I actually paid for the pain that's been inflicted on me. It's not facial peeling, it's facial blowtorching – I feel like I've been sandblasted. Thing is, it does look really good – all glowy and new (and that's not just because it's raw). They persuaded me to buy those creams and lotions made by Le Plateau. Altogether they cost a fortune – £115, but that's what was left over from the loan so it's not like I *really* spent one hundred and fifteen pounds of proper money, is it? Apparently they 'form the vital after-care maintenance crucial to sustaining the rejuvenating effect of a facial peel'. Well, that's what it says on the package. So apart from the stinging sensation when I go out, I'm sure it's worth it, it'll probably take years off me. When it all calms down, I'm sure at least some of my wrinkles will have disappeared, they must have, there's nowhere for them to live now. Gave Old Mrs M. a bit of a shock, she kind of yelped when I popped in to see her, she said that she'd thought something had exploded in my face. She's overreacting, it's just a bit red ... I think, God, I hope it will have calmed down by Monday, I can't possibly go into work if not.

12 October

Rang Sally to tell her about my facial peel and she said she couldn't wait to see it, so she rushed round. She thought that once the fell-asleep-under-a-sunlamp-look had subsided it would look really good. She was dead impressed with all my new Le Plateau cosmetics. We had a really nice day, spent most of it trying to decide, all in all, whether taken as a whole range Clinique, Clarins or Le Plateau was best. Finally agreed that whichever you get it's one of the few products where the more money you spend the more value and satisfaction you get.

13 October

My birthday. Had lunch with Mr Bowyer who said how pleased the company had been with my work on the Pozzi conferences. Apparently, Carlo Pozzi had been particularly complimentary about my skills (no trace of a knowing smirk from Bossy Bowyer when he said this). Got a card at work from Thin Clare and New Secretary Sarah. Mmm, don't know quite what to make of this. They evidently didn't think I was worth them both buying me a card, so decided to split the hefty £1.10 between them. Having dinner with Sal and Dan tonight ... re-enacting my role as gooseberry fool – again.

NB: Face still looks a bit florid but more red-like-I'm-permanently-embarrassed rather than hot-red-like-I'm-having-an-early-menopause, so not too bad.

14 October

When I got home yesterday, the post had arrived and there was a card from Andy! I didn't know he'd known when my birthday was. It just said, 'Hope all's well, love, Andy.' Oh yeah, and happy birthday, obviously. Can he possibly still have feelings for me? Out with Sally and Lovely Dan, couldn't think about anything except the card all night. When I asked Dan what he thought it meant, he said, 'A bloke wouldn't send a girl a birthday card unless he still really, really liked her ... or unless he was completely over her, had no feelings for her at all, but wanted to stay being polite and friendly.'

NB: I suppose racing up to Edinburgh, knocking on Andy's front door and shouting 'Surprise' through the letterbox, encouraged only by a birthday card, might be a bit much ... well, at this stage anyway. Sally thought it wasn't a bad idea, but Lovely Dan said, 'Better still, why not just ring him up, thank him for the card, tell him you've bought the wedding dress and ask him what he thinks about matching rings?' ... I think he was joking. Still, a card doesn't give much of an indication of anything, does it, really? I probably shouldn't start making total life-changing arrangements based on one decent gesture from Andy. Not like I did with PP – God, it makes my buttocks clench with embarrassment, remembering the complete twit I made of myself with no more encouragement than a nod of the head from that Lying Pig.

NB: All the same, clenching buttocks for any reason is good exercise.

Mum excelled herself this time. Her present was a pre-paid voucher for a self-esteem course she'd seen advertised in a woman's magazine, with a card saying, 'I thought this might interest you, hope you learn something.' Dad actually managed to send a card which arrived on the day, but the effect of him remembering the right date was somewhat undermined by the enclosure. It was a clipping from a newspaper about some girl I'd vaguely known at business college, who is now running her own company with a turnover of over £1.5 million a year. Precisely the sort of information you welcome any day of the year, natch, but on your birthday it certainly has an extra-special piquancy to it! Despite the parental assaults, the card from Andy made me feel absolutely great – hope I'm not overreacting.

16 October

Spent most of today *not* collating the information for my chart, which is supposed to be finished by the end of year, but composing potential e-mails to Andy. It took ages because I was trying to find exactly the right tone to sound relaxed, chatty and not too think-about-you-day-and-night-ish. Thing is, you can't really thank someone for a birthday card, it's not a very good excuse for making contact and I suppose I'd better stick to the Never Initiate Contact rule. I'll have to think of a very, very good reason to get in touch ... mmm, I wonder if he left anything in his desk, like an old pencil sharpener or some paper-clips (well, he *might* need them up there).

19 October

Eeeeek! Bossy Bowyer has invited me to dinner at his house

and on a weekend! Oh God, I can't bear it, I *knew* it was a mistake to do my job well. It's just that it's really hard hitting the right balance between being so crap at your job that you get the sack and so good that bosses start inviting you for games of golf and stuff and then expecting you to do even better. It's actually very difficult maintaining a constant state of mediocrity – which is obviously the best place to be because nobody ever notices you there. Mr Bowyer said that he and his wife, Cynthia (Cynthia Bowyer, could that sound more like a scary maths teacher?), were having some people to dinner that he'd like me to meet. People he'd like me to meet! People he'd like me to meet! Oh, yes, I can just imagine, probably a small selection of your basic top-drawer executives, nuclear scientists and world leaders, all of them sporting slim, beautiful wives. They will *all* have been at major universities having graduated with Alpha Betas, Capa Matas, Vauxhall Astras or whatever those extra-special degree grades are called, and words like 'genre', 'esoteric', 'râison d'être' and 'pusillanimous' will be being seamlessly blended into the conversation all over the shop. I'll still be stuck on 'esoteric' by the time the whole table has started talking in Middle English about Chaucer. Thing is, I can't say no, though, can I? I *could* injure myself – obviously it would have to be quite badly – or donate a major organ or something. Oh, I have to accept, I have to, if I make an excuse I'll probably find that my P45 has been biked round to my house and nailed to the front door before I get home. There is absolutely nothing in that *34 Steps* book about how to say no, I doubt very much whether they cater for that eventuality, I suppose it might not apply anyway as I'm not trying to stop Bossy Bowyer proposing to me, I'm just trying to get him to go off the idea of having me over for dinner.

NB: Downstairs Man bought a new Saab convertible recently,

I wonder if there's any chance he'd lend it to me to go to the Bowyers' house in. Slight risk involved in this as Mr Bowyer knows perfectly well I can't afford a car like that; however, there is the possibility that it would make the other guests think I was interesting and Mr and Mrs Bowyer might just think I'd got a rich, successful boyfriend. Mmm, just realised I don't know if the Bowyers have a house with a drive, because if they don't the whole Saab scam would be a complete waste of time. No, I'd have to be sure I could park the car right in front of the dining room. Also, I'd have to think of a very good reason to borrow the car off Downstairs Man too . . . oh dear, maybe it's all a bit labyrinthine (just looked that word up, it means complicated but I thought I'd better start getting used to using those kinds of words in an everyday sort of way so that they sound natural if I have to use them at the Bowyers').

4 a.m. – oh my God, it's just occurred to me, Bowyer hasn't invited me so that I can serve drinks and canapes, has he? Maybe I'd better wear black and take an apron so that I'm prepared and don't look like I think I was invited as a guest if he hands me a tray when I arrive.

21 October

Something really weird has happened. Thin Clare came up to me at work today and told me she'd been contacted by someone she'd been at university with (oh, just knew she'd have gone to a university) who is now the marketing manager for a magazine consortium.

Apparently this woman, Rachel Lowe, has asked Thin Clare for some suggestions for suitable women to feature in the first issue of a new magazine they are launching. Thin Clare thinks I'd be perfect and wanted to know if it was OK to suggest me. Mmm, I wonder why she isn't suitable? Perhaps this new magazine is called *On the Shelf* or *Fat Spinsters*.

23 October

Saw Foghorn in the hall this evening when I came back in from work, she was all friendly and normal. I guess that means that she doesn't know there was any connection between me and the Lying Pig her friend is now married to.

NB: I suppose, also, it's now safe to assume that I wasn't the punchline in the best man's speech at Lying Pig's wedding – God, I'd had nightmares about that.

NNB: I guess Foghorn and Downstairs Man are living together properly now – that explains why I never hear rampant sex any more.

25 October

That magazine woman, Rachel Lowe, called me today. I don't know whether to be flattered, humiliated, or just to push Thin Clare down the lift shaft. The new magazine is called *Spare Tyre* and the feature is on 'larger women in business'. I wished I'd been able to say, 'Actually, there's been a mistake. You see, Clare and I work on different floors and I've slimmed down to 6 stone since she last saw me.' Obviously I wasn't qualified to say that, but I did manage to mutter something about not being sure I could be described as being a 'large' woman – gosh, first time I've ever said something like that out loud. Rachel insisted that the magazine was aimed at ordinary-sized women who are sick and tired of seeing publications filled with pictures of anorexic schoolgirls, and that its readership isn't going to be 'huge, fat, ugly women with eating disorders' ... mmm, maybe not, but still, she had said 'larger women in business'.

I didn't want to sound defensive but I was very keen to establish exactly what she meant by 'larger'. After I'd pressed her further, Rachel said, 'Well, *Spare Tyre* is simply aimed at any and all women who are over a size 14 and have got a sense of humour.' She still hadn't given me a really satisfactory definition of 'larger' but I decided that pressing her to give me her and all of her co-workers' dress sizes would look too neurotic. Eventually I agreed to meet her without committing myself to being featured ... mmm, I wonder what I'm letting myself in for.

NB: Why would their target readership need a sense of humour? Be on the lookout for that when you meet this Rachel person.

27 October

Came home from work, managed not to go past McDonald's, so rewarded myself with a whole evening's TV watching. How many Oprah shows can you get in one night? Talk about fluctuating weight! They ought to theme her shows according to her size, like *Oprah – the Porky Years, Oprah – the Heavy*

Dieting years, Oprah – the HUMONGOUS years. Why can't she just stay one size – like that Vanessa Felch woman, doesn't seem to do her any harm.

28 October

Bumped into Thin Clare as I was leaving work, she gamely bowled up to me, all cheerful and normal. 'I hear you're going to meet Rachel, that's great. I really envy you, I'd love to do something like that. Unfortunately there was no chance of me being featured in the magazine.' All this with absolutely no hint of shame or embarrassment! I was just about to disembowel her with my umbrella when a thought suddenly popped into my head – could it be that Thin Clare didn't mean anything by it? Could it be that she'd suggested me because I am over a size 14 (well, only just, and not always)? Could it be . . . could it possibly be . . . that she doesn't think there's anything wrong with being over a size 14? Could she really, genuinely, truly envy me? Is it possible that she could hate being so thin (she is very thin, almost bony)? How could anyone, anywhere, envy a hefty person? Oh, I'm dreaming, it isn't possible, I'll never believe that, no matter what anyone says, never in my heart of hearts.

29 October

The soirée at the domicile of the person to whom I am under

employ falls upon tomorrow. I must say my anticipation is somewhat tremulous while at the same time, *ipso facto*, excitable.

Mmm, I don't think that sounds like I went to Oxford or Cambridge. I tried practising it with Old Mrs M. – that was a mistake, she couldn't keep a straight face and said I sounded like I was from one of those awful Jane Austen films. Perhaps I'd better stick to the way I speak normally, or better still just not talk at all, people always think other people that don't talk very much are interesting and deep, rather than boring and stupid, don't they?

31 October

Not one of the evenings that will be flashing before my eyes if I ever drown. Got to the Bowyers' at 8.15 p.m, mercifully I wasn't the first or last, so that was a weight off my mind, I'd timed it just right for once. Bossy Bowyer and his even bossier (but not bossy in an obvious way, she's controlling and dominating in a way that lets men think they rule the roost but it's really the woman who wears the trousers) wife live in one of those houses that sort of look old but can't be that old – Tudory on the outside and modern on the inside. They did have a drive but only a small one and their car was already in that, so it was lucky I didn't come in Downstairs Man's car because to get the full benefit, I'd have had to find some excuse to get them to move their car, and seeing as it was their drive that might have looked a bit rude. I wasn't given a tray of drinks when I went in, so the precautionary apron stayed put in my handbag (which was bulging a bit as a result, I hope no one thought I'd brought my pyjamas, thinking it was a sleep-over).

The other guests were not exactly petrifyingly glamorous (or in fact that slim) and not a world leader in sight. There was: a male colleague of Mrs Bowyer's from the school she teaches at and his wife, James and Alison Preed (I think it was Preed, sounds a bit unlikely now, though), and a neighbour of the Bowyers', David Manders, who was married but alone because his wife was 'visiting her mother'. He must have mentioned that about three times, unnecessarily frequently in my view, I'm sure he kept bringing her up to make it clear to me that he wasn't the 'available bloke at a dinner party' – like, being single, I was naturally going to pounce on him and he would have to subject me to some embarrassing, horrible rebuff. I couldn't think what I was doing there. As the evening wore on (and I mean wore) it dawned on me that Bossy Bowyer's wife wasn't very nice to him. Every time he said something, or poured out wine, or helped himself to vegetables or anything, she'd break off whatever she was saying and give him a sort of 'exactly what the hell do you think you're doing' face. She was one of those people who say 'darling' every time they speak to their husbands but always between gritted teeth, so instead of sounding like a term of endearment it sounds like 'you steaming piece of shit'. Bossy Bowyer was in the middle of talking to me and David Manders and suddenly she said, 'Darling, are you sure everyone's alright for wine,' but it really sounded like 'Look, you halfwit, do I have to do every single thing myself?' I came home wondering if I'd been invited because I was the only person Mr Bowyer could think of who would match the dullness of tonight's other guests, but then I realised that actually he probably isn't allowed to have many of his own friends outside her jurisdiction and that was his pathetic attempt at some sort of rebellion – a gues she hadn't vetted. I've decided that I feel really sorry for Mr B. and like him much more now that I've seen he's married to a drill sergeant.

NB: Distinct disadvantage to new feelings of pity for Bowyer – now that I feel sorry for him it's going to be much harder at work because whatever he asks me to do I'll say yes to because I'll feel that it's now my duty to make his life nicer. I always do that sort of thing, like when I read that Sainsbury's profits had dropped I felt all upset for them and went there to do a big shop even though I didn't need to.

1 November

That wretched self-esteem course is next weekend. Great, just can't wait. It's gone all cold now which means that I'll be wearing warm clothes which will make me look twice the size I really am when I go into the course, and everyone will think that's why I'm there. On the other hand maybe everyone will be thinking do people with small bums have low self-esteem?

3 November

Met that Rachel Lowe for lunch today, she was very cleverly dressed, I couldn't quite work out whether she was fat or thin. Her hands weren't fat and nor was her face, but then neither are mine, so that's not a hard and fast way of confirming a person's chunkiness. The main thing is she isn't six foot tall, and stick-thin. Apparently her company think that there's a market for a magazine focused on ordinary women in everyday life and using normal-sized models (i.e. 14–18 – that's normal?).

She wants to do an article on women who have jobs where image plays a part but isn't crucial to the success of the job. It would be on me, a sales manager in a clothes shop and an air hostess (I don't think I've ever seen a fat air hostess).

Actually, I quite like the idea of being in a magazine, talking about how difficult and important my job is, like people always do in magazine articles. But I'm not mad about the idea of identifying myself, in print, as someone who is officially 'larger'. Won't it be like hanging a sign around my neck that says 'IN CASE YOU HAVEN'T NOTICED, I AM FAT'? If you don't acknowledge it then you're not doing it, isn't that what alcoholics say – sounds like a very good rule of thumb to me.

4 November

Saw Mr Bowyer at work today, thanked him for the dinner and gave him a card to give to his wife, thanking her. I'd written it out 17 times before I thought it looked alright. I was terrified she might send it back with notes in red pen pointing out what was wrong with my grammar, or correcting my way of thanking someone. Poor old Bowyer, I'm surprised she doesn't send an invigilator to oversee his work at Pellet's.

5 November

Nearly e-mailed Andy to tell him about going to Bowyer's for dinner but then decided against it – he might think I was showing off or having an affair with him or start worrying about me being promoted.

Talked to Sally, she thinks this magazine article thing is a great idea, she would though, wouldn't she? She said, 'Look, you're not fat. Alright, you're not Kate Moss, but you represent the normal size of three-quarters of the women in this country, or some huge statistic like that. Anyway, it'll be a laugh!' Maybe, but a laugh for who? That's what I'm worried about. My mum will ring up and say something about not being able to hold her head up in the hairdresser's, and how do I think it feels to have a daughter proud to publicly link herself to the rightly reviled silent majority of 'larger' women? She'd probably prefer it if I became a member of the IRA, at least their members' names are kept secret. Better to be a bomber than a fattie.

Oh, I should agree to do it for two reasons: a) no one will see it and b) it'd be silly to pass up an opportunity to annoy Mum like that.

6 November

Rang Rachel Lowe up and said I'd do the article. Felt really strange and not-in-my-own-bodyish after that. It was almost as if I'd accepted myself as I am in some way ... wow, I wonder if that's what self-respect feels like.

9 November

Really had to drag myself out of bed yesterday morning, the self-esteem thing started at 9 a.m. and was halfway across town. I didn't want to be late, because then everyone would look at me when I went in. It was being held in some grim institutional building, with loads of rooms filled with people wearing those awful cloth shoes doing that Chinese thing that looks like you're directing traffic. I think it's called Tai Chi, or To Fu or Tie Dyed or something. Took me ages to find the room the self-esteem course was in, I didn't want to ask anyone where it was, I thought that would just look too pathetic. Anyway, did get lost and managed to be the last one, so, of course, everyone *did* look at me. I hovered sort of half in and half out of the door for what felt like two years and considered legging it while a room full of people sitting in chairs in a circle all stared blankly at me. Eventually the leader, Bernard (you'd need really good self-esteem to be called Bernard), extended his hand to indicate the one remaining empty chair; I slunk in and sat down. Then Bernard indicated to under our chairs where there was some card and a marker pen which apparently we had to pick up. On his he'd written, 'Write your name and what you think you lack on the card. Then hold it up on your lap. No speaking at this stage.' Just like that? No gentle easing in? No coffee and a little chit-chat before we lay ourselves bare to total strangers? Had I missed a bit? I was only fifteen minutes late. I couldn't believe we were being thrown in at the deep end without so much as a pair of water wings. I was so terrorised by this instruction that I briefly thought of writing on mine, 'I have a large quantity of Semtex strapped to my body, leave the room immediately or I will detonate the charge' so that the hell could end there and then. Decided against it when I realised that having been late I'd probably already qualified to be the example Bernard was going to use to illustrate the 'Inappropriate ways of getting attention' item on the agenda. Eventually I decided that seeing as everyone else had to do it as well then it might not be too bad. I couldn't decide on any one specific thing I lacked, so eventually I just put 'Jacqueline M. Pane – Everything'. That was my first big mistake. I definitely should have gone for the Semtex. Every single person in there had evidently done 80 million of these types of courses before and could write books on what they lacked, if required. When I'd finished my card and held it up, I looked round the room and it was all 'Jonathan – the courage to claim my own space within a relationship', 'Marcia – the ability to feel special and unique in the proper context' and 'Harold – the confidence to reward myself for my individuality'. By the time I'd finished reading all the cards I felt like an alien. How come they all knew what to do? I started panicking that I'd got the wrong room, I'd joined a class in advanced self-indulgence. After Bernard had indicated that we should put our cards down he finally spoke (and what a surprise, he turned out to be American) and told us we were going to play a 'status game'. He gave us each cards with numbers between 1 and 10 on them and told us not to tell anyone else what our number was but to go around the room talking to each other the way that we thought the number we'd got would behave and try and work out what other people's numbers were. Mum had found another brilliant way to torture me, but this time cleverly disguised as a present. I got a 6 – I didn't know what a bloody number 6 behaves like so I waited to see how the other people were behaving and set my status according to theirs. That's probably not a very high-self-esteemy way to behave, is it? I don't think you're supposed to be constantly measuring yourself against others. Well, it wasn't a test and I didn't want to go about being all middle-management and obsequious (which is what I suppose a 6 would be like) and then find that everyone else was a 10. Anyway, it was probably quite 6-ish to wait and see what everyone was doing first. We broke for lunch after that, none the wiser what number everyone else had got except for Harold who I think must have got a 1 because he'd just sat in a corner crying while we were doing the game. In the café, some fantastically good-looking girl plopped herself down next to me. I couldn't remember what her card had revealed which turned out not to be a problem because when she started talking to me she told me that her real problem wasn't the inability to decide (as she'd put on her card) but really it was believing that men liked her for herself not just her looks and body but that she couldn't fit all of that on to her card – oh, for the love of God. What a trial her life must be.

After lunch, we spent the afternoon doing painfully embarrassing exercises which mainly consisted of constructing positive sentences to describe ourselves. Each sentence had to include a word Bernard had given us like 'deserve, individual, earned, beautiful, special' . . . etc., etc. I started yearning for the cards, they were an infinitely better option. This exercise was to be done sitting in the circle again and saying our sentences out loud, one after the other! Dear God in heaven, I thought I was going to die of shame. Naturally not one person in that group had the slightest difficulty blending their allotted words into their proclamations: 'I deserve to be treated with greater respect at work' and 'I am a beautiful person who has earned the right to be with someone who sees my internal beauty.' When it was my turn I couldn't think of anything to say except things like 'I don't get individual portions at the supermarket' or 'If I was beautiful life would be perfect' – and judging by the look of complete horror on everybody's faces I don't think I got the gist of the game. At the end of the day we all had to line up so Bernard could hug us goodbye. I wasn't exactly relishing the prospect of his hug, I mean, he was three foot tall and smelt like a pet shop, but still I was petrified that he would withhold my hug because I'd so obviously failed to markedly raise my self-esteem. I don't know if he could tell, though. His parting gift to each of us was a chant that he'd come up with tailored to everyone's particular needs, he said. Mine was – 'I am a significant, precious person with a lot to offer'. Apparently I'm supposed to say this to myself whenever I am feeling low. Hey, why keep it to myself? Why not share this great news with the bus conductor, at the sandwich bar, in the middle of a meeting? Oh yes, I can just see me making time in my daily schedule to repeat that every time I feel low – there wouldn't be any time left in the day to say anything else. On second thoughts, I am going to say it but once and once only – when I ring Mum to thank her for enriching my life with the wonderful gift of self-esteem, I'm going to have a field day. She won't be able to criticise me because it was all her idea in the first place, oh, heaven, it was all worth it now that I've thought of that.

10 November

Got home and there were no messages on the answerphone except one from Sally and one from the dry cleaner's wanting to know if some purple trouser suit that's been left there for over three months is mine – a purple trouser suit? Very likely indeed, maybe that's their idea of a joke.

Felt all pissed off, don't know why, I suppose I sort of always hope deep down inside that there'll be a message from Andy. Obviously I do 1471 as soon as I get in the door but often don't recognise the number, and then end up wasting hours going through the phone book trying to find a phone number that matches which is probably all a bit of a waste of time. Mind you, it gives me something to do of an evening.

12 November

Work is fine, bit boring. Keen John Weston isn't quite as irritating as he was when he first started, although he is constantly bringing me new little bits of information for my chart. Yesterday he brought me a list of good restaurants within a six-mile radius of the Aberdeen conference venue! I know it's a good idea to have as much information as you can about the surrounding area but his dedication is endless. It just makes me feel like doing nothing all day except doodless and composing e-mails to Andy that I'm never going to send. When other people around me are all filled with vim and vigour it doesn't fire me up, it just makes me feel all floppy and useless.

Bossy B. told me that Carlo Pozzi wants to do another series of conferences early next year, including one in Italy. I guess that's a good sign, isn't it? I mean he obviously isn't that annoyed with me, is he? Unless Carlo's going to make some special stipulation that I can't have anything to do with them. Oh dear. No, he can't have been that keen on me.

NB: Just realised that in cases like the above, where I am the object of unwanted attention, the *Spare Tyre* article could be a good way of putting people off me without having to reject them directly myself.

Oh, listen to me, 'put people off me' – people! people! Yeah, like the future holds a gaggle of gorgeous, sane PNBs battling to be near me!

14 November

Keen John Weston must die. I went into work early this morning so I could catch up on stuff that had been delayed due to excessive time spent doodling. No one else was in and I was just settling down to it when I noticed that my e-mail thing was flashing. My heart nearly leapt out of my mouth. I suppose foolishly, now that I think about it, but you never know, anyway, it doesn't matter now, but I was absolutely convinced it was going to be a letter from Andy – I couldn't think who else would have e-mailed me between last night and early this morning. But it wasn't from Andy, oh no, not at all, it was something much more interesting than that, it was an e-mail from John that he'd sent from his house, telling me he'd spoken to a relative in Aberdeen and apparently one of the restaurants on the list he gave me isn't as good as it used to be and he'd like to take that one off and will let me know as soon as he gets a replacement! What is that man trying to do to me? How could he imagine that I needed that information urgently? Maybe it's all a plot to drive me out of my mind and while I'm recovering in a high-security asylum, he can slip into my place and show everyone just how easily he can juggle my job and his. Keen John had better be careful, though – he may have died in a freak industrial accident before he's able to do that.

15 November

Woke up in the middle of the night feeling guilty about Keen John. I must, must be more tolerant, otherwise people might realise how I feel about him which will inevitably make them pity and like him more than me and then lead to their spotlight turning on me and they'll start thinking, 'Yeah, well, maybe he is a bit keen but at least he makes an effort and just how fascinating and vital is every bit of work you do, then, if you think you're in a position to piss on him from a great height?'

17 November

The journalist from *Spare Tyre* is coming to meet me in a couple of days – what on earth am I going to wear? Will it look odd if I've had a full professional body and face makeover from the Clarins counter?

19 November

Too early to send Andy a Christmas card?

22 November

Rachel Lowe and her photographer came to work today to do the interview. Mr Bowyer seemed quite pleased about me doing this, I'm worried that he may think it's good publicity for the company. He probably thinks it makes Pellet's look all equal opsy, you know, like 'Look at us, we employ all types, even slightly overweight women, we must be a right-on, radical-thinking company'. It was all fairly straightforward, just like having a chat, really. She didn't ask me loads of 'large'-orientated questions or anything hideous like that. She just treated me as if I was completely normal and asked the sort of questions about the job that most people ask about organising conferences. The photographer took some photos of me at my desk and on the phone. I made sure there were no shots of me walking down the hall or standing up or anything awful like that. I may be in an article about 'larger women', but it doesn't have to include a rear-view photo of me to drive the point home. Can't wait to see the article . . . I think.

23 November

Keen John fixed that bit on my Anglepoise lamp today – he is driving me nuts. I hadn't asked him to do it, he'd just 'happened to notice that it was sagging a bit'! God, he's like bloody Superman! Pity he's not a plastic surgeon as well, he'd be more useful to me fixing other things that he just 'happened to notice were a bit saggy'.

24 November

Broke a heel on the way home from work. How embarrassing is that? Particularly seeing as I did that thing of carrying on walking along without realising that one of the heels had dropped off. I must have looked like a right idiot. It's only second down the list of 'most embarrassing things that can happen' next to going out with yesterday's knickers or pop-sock wedged halfway down one trouser leg all day and not noticing until you get undressed at the end of the day . . . I can't be the only person who's done that, can I? The good thing is that as long as the item stays lodged in the same place all day then there's a good chance if someone did see it they'd think it was a tumour and not say anything.

To round off my fabulous day there was a note pushed under my front door from Downstairs Man, when I came home tonight, saying, 'We need to have a chat soon about the state of the drains.' What's all that about? The state of the drains? The state of the drains? I haven't noticed anything wrong with the drains. What is he trying to suggest? When people say things like 'the state of' whatever it is they are talking about 'the state of', what they *really* mean is that they think you're responsible for 'the state of' whatever it is. The clear implication of his note is that I've deliberately done something which has resulted in 'the state of' the drains which now needs discussing. I'll bet this is all leading to him trying to get me to pay a greater proportion of the cost of seeing to 'the state of' the drains.

25 November

Crept out of the flat this morning at 6.30 a.m. I know it's a bit weedy and I am going to stand my ground with Downstairs Man over his false accusations of my having sabotaged the drainage system but I just wasn't up to it this morning.

26 November

Woke up really early again this morning, it's amazing how hard it is to get to sleep when you haven't eaten. I couldn't use the kitchen in case Downstairs Man heard and decided that was the best moment to confront me. When I came home from work all his lights were off, but he might have been trying to catch me off guard and I'm still not quite ready to face him. I *am* going to deal with this problem but I just want to get my defence fully together before he attacks me with all the arguments he's been building up. He's had more time to put together his case than me, remember, he's the one who thought of all this in the first place.

27 November

This whole drain issue is making me very tense. Maybe I should just face the music and get the whole thing over and done with. I don't even know what he's going to say and I already feel like I've done something wrong. I bet he'll try and humiliate me into agreeing to the work by suggesting that perhaps I have heavier periods than Foghorn does and maybe use more sanitary protection, or maybe that I go to the lavatory more as I eat more and therefore use more loo paper, or that seeing as I wear more make-up than she does I must surely use the sink more often to wash it off. His flat is much bigger than mine, so if anyone should be paying a greater proportion of any works needed to the outside of the house it should be him, not me. As it is I'll probably be contributing towards Old Mrs M.'s share and I don't see why I should fork out for more than Downstairs Man. In fact, as he has a girlfriend living with him there's every argument for *him* paying the largest proportion by far, after all, there's two of them. He's obviously got lots of spare cash, the new car being evidence of that. Oh, help, things were going fine between us until now, I hardly ever saw him it's true, and I suppose I never complimented him on the new Saab . . . oh God, and I never gave them a good luck card when she moved in, but they're hardly capital offences, just maybe a bit thoughtless. I mean, as it is I look after Old Mrs M., he never lifts a finger when it comes to her, does he? Oh no. And you don't catch me pushing note after note under his door saying things like 'Would you help me change her sheets next week', do you? So why has he suddenly started haranguing me night and day about the drains? Well, whatever his reasons, I'm not having it. I will not be cowed into submission in my own home. Enough's enough, if it's a fight he wants then he's got one.

28 November

Came home in full fighting spirit and decided tonight was the night to tackle Downstairs Man. I dumped my stuff in the flat and went down, I was just about to hammer his door down (I thought he might be hiding) when he comes in the main door and says breezily, 'How are you? Long time no see.' He starts merrily chatting away about this and that. Course, I didn't hear a word, seeing as I was already at boiling point when I'd left my flat, so, not being able to stand the pressure a moment longer, just as I was about to explode with built-up tension, I blurt out, 'Look, I got your note and really resent the implication that I am less feminine and ladylike than Fog . . . erm . . . Tory . . . and therefore likely to be responsible for the current state of the drains, ye gods, it's not as if I haven't got enough on my plate as it is what with Keen John driving me round the bend and the sodding chart to complete by the end of the year and not so much as a peep from Attractive New Andy. Please just get off my back.' With that I stormed off upstairs, leaving him standing in the hall doing an impressive imitation of a carp. It took me hours to calm down and that wasn't until after I'd let off a bit of steam by ringing up the ITV switchboard to complain about them rescheduling *Peak Practice* for some crappy old football match. Thing is that *was* quite annoying but actually going through with the phone call was probably a bit unhinged, wasn't it? That's the sort of thing people with really empty lives do all day long, I'm sure.

29 November, 5 a.m.

Oh my God . . . I've woken up in a cold sweat, I had a terrible dream – I was taken away in an ambulance in a straitjacket and then I arrived at this enormous white hospital and the doctor waiting for me was Downstairs Man and then he did that electric shock thing on my head and my tongue was hanging out of my mouth and I couldn't speak, it was horrible. It's just dawned on me – Downstairs Man didn't say anything about the drains or in fact anything at all that deserved that outburst, I've just realised the full extent of what I said to him. He must think I'm stark raving mad, for all I know the drains problem had been solved, after all there's been no mention of it since he left the note. I cannot believe I did that, it's lucky I didn't have a gun, I'd probably have shot him if he'd tried to answer back. I am going to have to think of a *brilliant* explanation as to why I flew off the handle. 'Demise of a relative' probably a bit risky as one of them might turn up here one day, 'loss of job' makes me look tragic. I know, I'll look up some things that can happen to the brain, see if any of them will do ... mmm, I wonder if I could say I'd had a mini-stroke.

I'll have to avoid him until I've thought of something feasible.

30 November

Mr Bowyer asked me if I thought asking Keen John and Thin Clare (he doesn't call them that, obviously) to organise this year's Christmas party was a good idea. I said it was a very good idea – refrained from adding that her idea of seasonal fare would probably be a tray of Ryvitas, topped with cottage cheese and a raw vegetable garnish, washed down with some low-cal wine, and his idea of party games would be a company lap around the nearest racetrack.

1 December

Keith rang today to talk about plans for Christmas. I guess it'll be the usual 48 hours of living hell at Mum's, but at least with Keith, the prodigal son, there I won't be the focus of much attention.

2 December

Bumped straight into Downstairs Man on my way out this morning, very solicitously and gently he says, 'Are you alright?' – in that way you talk to people who are crying at bus stops. I was so mortified. I said, 'Oh yes, absolutely fine now, look, I'm really sorry about that fit I had, you see I'd just had an embolism.' It was the first thing that popped into my head. Well, someone had had it in *Casualty* last week and they hadn't died, just acted a bit weird. I'm not sure exactly what an embolism is but I know it's to do with the head, so that could cover why someone would do something peculiar like shout at their neighbour, couldn't it? He gave me a kind of puzzled 'oh, right' look and then said, 'Well, take care of yourself, let us know if you need anything.'

NB: Look up 'embolism'. I might have confessed to some awful venereal disease.

3 December

Saw Sally and Lovely Dan this evening. They've set a firm date for their wedding at last, next 12 April. Sally has asked me to be matron of honour, she insists that is the correct name for the chief bridesmaid. Don't like it much, I must say. After a little pressure, Sally agreed to a verbal contract confirming there would be no discussion of peach/cream/pale pink/pale yellow or any pastels for bridesmaids' outfits. She dug her heels in, though, when I mooted black or navy as an option

– God, it's not like she has to wear it. Told Dan that I hadn't heard from Andy since the birthday card. First off, Dan asked if I could be sure he wasn't dead. I said I knew he wasn't because a couple of people in the office are in contact with him about things he's still dealing with. Sally annoyingly interrupted at this stage to point out, completely unnecessarily in my view, that it wasn't a particularly good sign that he was talking to people in the office but not asking after me. I was really pleased because obviously this had occurred to me but Dan said he didn't think that was a bad sign because probably, like most blokes, Andy doesn't want anyone else to think he has any special reason to ask after me – or, alternatively, he doesn't ask about me because he's completely forgotten I exist. I never know whether Dan's teasing me or telling me like it is from a man's point of view, or rather eunuch's point of view in terms of me and him.

NB: Andy can't have forgotten I exist, can he? For a start my name is among those printed on most of the memos he gets.

4 December

'Embolism – the blockage to a blood vessel, usually heart, lungs or brain . . . can result in sudden death.' Well, obviously not in this case, but it probably wasn't a brilliant choice now that I know what it actually means, but still, a small one might make you throw a wobbly, like the one I subjected Downstairs Man to. He isn't very likely to know *exactly* what it is and unless he's really suspicious he won't look it up . . . will he?

NB: Just to be on the safe side I'd better mention that it was a minor one next time I see him.

5 December

NB: Do not wear any red or green or brown to work in run-up to Christmas – could encourage comments about elfs and reindeers from the boys in the production department.

6 December

Saw Dad and Jennifer for supper tonight. I do declare, I think Jennifer was actually a little jealous about me being in a magazine article (naturally I didn't say what the magazine was called)! It felt brilliant.

7 December

Rang Sally to tell her that I'd looked up matron of honour, (did it at the same time as embolism) and it's *maid* of honour not matron . . . I thought it sounded a bit Barbara Windsory.

8 December

Dad rang me at work today and said that he and Jennifer had

been talking after I'd left the other night and had decided how nice it would be to have a family pre-Christmas dinner all together – me, them, Keith, Bee and Kyle! Nice for who? As if the whole Yuletide thing isn't daunting enough as it is. The office party is fast approaching, it will probably turn out to be the event of the year, talked about in the office until the end of time, and become the benchmark by which all company events are measured thereafter. Up at Mum's, she will faint and swoon over every single present Keith gives her, while I'll be lucky if I get so much as a cursory thank you for mine. She'll have invited one of her disgusting old neighbours to Christmas lunch and he'll slip his gnarled old hand on to my knee under the table and tell me that there's 'life in the old goat yet'. And now, to top it all, I've got to have a festive meal and make conversation with my step-siblings who make me feel about as comfortable as walking round Sainsbury's with no clothes on.

NB: Possibly worth considering resurrection of glamorous, mysterious boyfriend for this dinner. Not sure I could count on Keith's support, though.

9 December

Haven't been to the gym for ages. I kind of think I don't *have* to go now. Like I've got a good reason – I've been in an article about 'larger women' so I can't do any more exercise in case I lose weight and don't qualify to be featured in the article by the time it comes out and then I might get stopped in the street by people saying, 'Oi, you shouldn't have been in that article.'

NB: Mmm, that sounds more like the sort of lame, really lengthy excuse we used to come up with at school to get off hockey practice.

10 December

Honestly, you'd think Keen John and Thin Clare had been asked to organise a NATO summit meeting. They're always huddling together in the canteen at lunch-time. It's not like it's that big a deal, really! Typical of those two to find a way to organise a poxy party that makes it seem like something worth doing *and* makes me feel left out. I didn't even want to organise it but it'd be nice if they occasionally asked me what I thought about decorations or something.

Dropped a Christmas card in at Downstairs Man's this evening, it said Merry Christmas and Happy New Year, obviously, that was printed on it, I signed it and then added a sort of casual, chatty postcript letting him know that the embolism had only been a minor one. That way if he *has* looked it up then I'm covered for tearing him off a strip and if he hasn't looked it up, it makes the whole episode seem run-of-the-mill and not worth him ever thinking about again or bringing up with me.

1 December

Got sent the first issue of *Spare Tyre* today, it's fantastic . . .

THE LADIES WHO ARE BIG BUSINESS
by Rachel Lowe

So does it matter any more? Who cares these days? Big is beautiful. We're fat and we're proud. That's what women all over the country are saying and who can blame them? In today's workplace it's not the Kate Moss look-alike anorexics that dominate, it's the full-bodied ordinary women that rule the roost. There are over 15,000 women in management positions today and 85% of them weigh over 12 stone, 65% of them wear over a size 16 – put together they weigh an impressive 2,142,000 pounds! This is something they're proud of. They don't see it as a bad thing, they don't even see it as a problem, they say a woman's weight shouldn't be, and isn't, or for them at any rate, an issue. They insist that gone are the days when only thin women could expect promotion, 'we bigger girls won't stand for being the dinner ladies any more'. All very well, but how does it affect their lives, their jobs? Do other people see it the same way? *Spare Tyre* has taken three women with important, high-profile jobs, where one might argue their body image plays a part. I talked to Geraldine Sessions, Manager of the 'Stop Right There' fashion stores, Shirley Stevens, Chief Air Stewardess on short-haul flights with Spartacus Airlines, and Jacqueline M. Pane, the Senior Conference Organiser for the Pellet Corporation. The four of us met up for a lavish lunch. I asked them what it was like holding down a difficult job *and* being larger than life. Geraldine, wearing a simple pale blue trouser suit, hotly maintained that size didn't feature in her job . . . 'I know I'm not skinny but I don't see that as being a problem. Three-quarters of women in Britain can't get into the majority of sizes available in the high streets. Why should only thin women know how to give advice on fashion? I have very good dress sense and can advise our customers, whatever their size, on what does and doesn't look good.' I asked her if she thought customers might be put off by her being overweight ... 'No, I don't think so, why should they be? I'm not telling them to be like me, I'm helping them choose the best clothes for them – whatever size they are. My customers range from size 8 to size 18 and I give the same advice across the board – is the outfit right for the occasion and do you look good in it?' Fighting talk and good for you, Geraldine, we certainly could do with more women like her in the fashion business. Shirley has a less combative attitude and sees the whole issue from a practical point of view ... 'As long as I can walk comfortably down the aisle while pushing the buffet trolley, I don't think my weight has, or should have, anything to do with how I do my job.' I asked Shirley if she ever worried that nervous passengers might blame her extra weight in the event of a plane crash ... 'I'm still below EU-stipulated poundage for airborne staff and the good thing about nervous passengers is that when we do encounter turbulence or bad weather, they're too busy having heart attacks to notice anything else!' What a great sense of humour Shirley has, and courage – lucky Shirl. I think most readers would agree, you'll always find those lovely qualities in us chunkier ladies! Jacqueline wasn't saying much during lunch, but I realised, as a conference organiser, she is the one with the most at stake – meeting new people, and making a good impression, is at the very core of her work, so her appearance must be of great concern. 'I think about it night and day, it's dominated my every waking thought and ruled my life like a pathological obsession,' Jackie burst out. Gosh, get a grip, Jacqueline, I found myself thinking. Jackie is by far the slimmest of the three, in fact she only just qualified to feature in this magazine. Maybe that's why she has the greatest difficulty in tackling the issue. In particular, Jackie seemed to be fixated by the size of her bottom. It isn't small but then again it isn't vast. Jackie also had the least positive attitude to life – I found myself wondering where was the defiance, the courage in the face of all odds, the ability to laugh at herself. The assets that Shirley and Geraldine have in such abundance. After the lunch was over, I found myself comparing these women and their lives – Shirley moving comfortably up the aisle *en route* to, say, Aberdeen, Geraldine doing her best not to accidentally-on-purpose help a slim girl choose something horrible and unflattering, and Jacqueline braving her way through conference after conference, meeting after meeting, plagued by the constant fear that she doesn't look quite right. Fleshy and ashamed, I don't think so, not any more. Goodbye Hattie Jacques, hello Roseanne and Clare Short – large and proud of it.

'Slimmest of the three', 'slimmest of the three', do you see that? 'Slimmest of the three', hallelujah, hallelujah, praise be to God on high! Someone has used, in print, for all the world to see, the word slimmest as an adjective to describe me. Me! I could jump for joy! For the rest of time (if it doesn't fade too badly) I have a printed document saying that I am slimmer than two other people! What a great article! Rachel Lowe is a genius, her writing is so incisive, so sincere, so evocative. Obviously she's improvised a bit with the truth – I didn't meet her for lunch and I didn't actually say any of that stuff (as if!), but who cares, it's a great article. I think I come off really well in it. I hope the whole of the nation buys *Spare Tyre* – it's great.

NB: Maybe I should get the article blown up, and highlight the 'Jackie is by far the slimmest of the three' bit and have it as a poster in my flat ... or perhaps there's a subtle way of incorporating that bit into my Christmas cards.

13 December

Feeling on top of the world. I am 'slimmest' out of three – and that's official.

14 December

Popped into see Mrs M. this evening. I've done something a bit rash, but I'm quite pleased. She told me that the community centre round the corner has cancelled the OAPs' Christmas lunch and that she's got no one to be with. I couldn't face the idea of leaving her on her own, particularly as I'd only be trudging up to Mum's to throw Keith's magnificence into relief, so I said I'd have Christmas with her. She was really pleased and thought we'd have a laugh, we probably will actually. I put my foot down about the *Street* Christmas special though, she didn't seem to mind.

16 December

I am actually enjoying the prospect of Christmas, now that I won't have to endure the sound of air being sucked in sharply every time I eat a mince pie.

NB: Better ring Mum and give her the glad tidings.

17 December

My word, wonders will never cease. A woman called Josie Mather rang me at work today and said she'd seen the article in *Spare Tyre* and wanted to know if I'd be interested in organising a series of conferences on 'Women and Self-Image' next spring. She's forming a women's group with sponsorship from places like the Body Shop, Evans Outsize and Overeaters Anonymous.

The group will take its membership principally from 'large' women with influential positions in the media, law, politics, etc. She said the group's aim is to encourage advertisers and the fashion and make-up industry, through conferences, seminars and sponsorship, to move away from the enforced perception that there is a 'right' shape and size for women in todays society.

Wow! How fantastic to be in a group where you actually *have* to be overweight, I mean, I suppose it is compulsory, it must be. Imagine a whole new world in which the size of a person's bum isn't the most important thing about them. If there really could be a paradise like that I'd be liberated from the chains that have shackled me all my life; probably not when I saw Mum or Dad, though – that would be too much to expect. I can't believe she wants me to be involved, I'm so flattered, I'm so terrified. It's all so grown up and mature! Thank God, she didn't ask to meet up yet, she only knows about me from the article, if she met me in real life she'd probably be really disappointed. I'll make sure I do loads of really impressive research before we ever meet so that there's a better chance of her staying wanting me involved when we finally meet. She's going to send me the background information on the whole thing. Initially everyone's involvement is on a voluntary basis, but after a while I'd probably have to leave Pellet's and go full time, if the whole thing takes off.

NB: Are there enough 'large' women with important jobs to make this thing really work – how could I check? I wonder if there's a kind of Fat Women's Directory anywhere ... mmm, maybe I should start one.

Rang Mum when I got home to tell her I wouldn't be coming up for Christmas. It'd be a little paranoid to say she whooped with joy, but fair to say she didn't exactly sound crushed. Can't have it both ways, I suppose. She did manage to claim credit for my decision, however, she said, 'Well, that self-esteem course I paid so much for must have worked if you feel emotionally secure enough to spend Christmas away from the bosom of your family.' I was about to start yelling and screaming down the phone, just as Mum intended, when I realised I had a much more effective reaction up my sleeve. I took a deep breath and said calmly, 'I am a significant, precious person with a lot to offer. Bye, Mum, talk to you soon.' She was speechless, her hen's arse mouth must have gone into overdrive!

NB: While a useful tool with which to wind up Mum, do not get drunk at Christmas office party and point out to selected heads of departments that 'I am a significant, precious blah, blah, blah ...'

19 December

Very worrying news – I tried on that black skirt today. I was going through a few outfit options for Dad's thing tomorrow, and it's practically falling off! Great, so now I lose weight. Fabulous timing as usual, I lose weight now, right now – when

I'm not trying to and it'll mean I won't qualify for the women's group thing. Oh, I'm sure I would be hugely popular, turning up to the first meeting looking sleek and streamline.

Maybe I'm running away with myself here, the black skirt is just a tiny bit looser, I haven't exactly turned into Olive Oyl. Still, better use tomorrow night as an excuse to stuff myself.

20 December

Is there no end to the embarrassment I have to endure? Does every aspect of my life *have* to spew out endless gobs of shame and humiliation? Can't there be one, just one, oasis offering peace and dignity? I have very mixed (I'm sure 'mixed' is what people say when they daren't say bad) feelings about the news announced at tonight's Christmas dinner with Dad and everyone. Oh, well. The whole clan was gathered at this alright-ish, bit poncey, waiters constantly whipping away your plate the moment you look like you'd finished, restaurant near Dad and Jennifer's. Things had been going OK, conversation not too stilted, a couple of potential rows had been diverted by Keith. There'd been one mighty uncomfortable moment, where Keith didn't help out, when Bee had asked me something about my journey to Lisbon from 'Mum and Ralph's' (I usually manage to forget my dad's called Ralph until I see that lot). I got this awful sinking feeling, I was sure that she knew I hadn't actually gone to Lisbon and was doing this deliberately. I panicked – I couldn't be sure she hadn't done the journey a million times herself, I didn't know how to avoid answering, so I opted for knocking over my glass of wine instead. In the ensuing kerfuffle, during which

I'm absolutely sure he heard Kyle tsk, Dad says, 'We've got something to tell you all.' My heart sank. God, what is it now? He's going to have a sex change, they've joined a religious cult, Jennifer's taking a job at Pellet's! But no, the truth was much, much worse, in fact much worse than those three possibilities all put together. Dad looked at Jennifer, she gave him one of those awful smiles, like Princess Diana was always doing before she wised up – those smiles that say, 'I'm only a little woman and defer to my great master' – then Dad turns to face us all and says, 'We're going to have a baby.' You could practically hear jaws cracking open – Keith, Bee, Kyle and I were dumbstruck. A baby! A baby! She's 45, he's 60 – what the bloody hell are they thinking of?! I couldn't take it in at all, for a minute I thought they *must* mean a baby dog, or baby cat, they couldn't possibly mean a human baby. There was a deafening silence from everyone, eventually broken by a sort of strangled wail from Bee. 'You've dominated my life from the moment I was born, you selfish old cow, and now you can't even bugger off to your bungalow in Portugal and grow old gracefully, you've got to carry on pretending you're 25!' It was then that I realised I liked Bee a lot more than I'd ever done before. Kyle wasn't saying anything but he did look like he'd sucked a lemon. So, it would appear that Jennifer and her perfect children don't have quite as harmonious a relationship as she would have you believe. Dad tried to rectify the situation. 'I know it must be hard for you all to accept but we want a child of our own and luckily it's still possible.' In a way, I can see why they'd want a child of their own, I mean, to date they've both buggered up the lives of two children apiece, this way they can combine their skills and see what effect they can have as a pair. The evening sort of ground crunchingly to a halt after that. Well, chat about the merits of sage-and-onion stuffing versus chestnut-and-prune doesn't seem to flow easily after that kind of bombshell. Keith gave me a lift home, we had a bit of a row on the way because he said he thought I should tell Mum; to which I replied, 'Over my dead body.' Keith said, 'But I never give Mum bad news, that's your job.' I'd never really thought about it before but it's true. Keith's all sunshine and smiles around Mum; well, time to face the music, little bro, she's armed and dangerous and I've already run for cover.

NB: I hope Dad doesn't think I'm going to do loads of baby-sitting.

22 December

Just got home from the office party, it was quite good actually, Keen John had organised some great dancing music. I'm not drunk, honestly, but I did trip on the stairs and I think I might have woken Downstairs Man up – serve him right. I did have a few drinks but not lots and lots and lots, there's probably a loose bit of carpet on the stair. I danced with Mr Bowyer tonight, he's quite a mover, I must say! Oh God, I must be drunk – if jigging about with Bossy Bowyer is worth a diary entry. Got to go now, byeeeeeeee. Night, night. Oh, help, I don't feel very well . . .

23 December, 7.20 a.m.

Oh God, oh God, never again. I promise, I will never, ever touch alcohol again as long as I live. I woke up this morning, sprawled across my bed, with all my clothes on – including my shoes! When I took them off my feet stayed in the shape of the shoes. I feel really queasy and I've got to do all my Christmas shopping today. Marvellous, I can't think of anything I'd rather do, except perhaps watch a documentary on the dissection of someone's internal organs.

4.45 p.m.

I am now in a position to warmly recommend shopping with a hangover in the last 48 hours before Christmas. Not only did I feel terrific, but this sense of well-being was added greatly to by the lovely Christmassy feeling exuding from my fellow shoppers and shop staff. I came within an inch of my life over the last jar of cranberry sauce and was virtually wrestled to the ground in M&S by an over-zealous store detective who'd decided that I was erroneously in the five-items-or-less queue.

24 December

Gosh, guess what, guess what? I can't believe it. During lunch-hour today, I went out for more guerrilla warfare, otherwise known as shopping on Christmas Eve, I didn't get everything yesterday, anyway, when I got back to the office Andy was there! He'd dropped in to say hi to everyone. Apparently he's down in London to spend Christmas with his parents. It was absolutely lovely to see him, I didn't have time to panic about the way I looked or anything. He was very friendly and nice to me. He came up at one point and said, 'I saw that article you were in, I thought you really stood out' – WOW! I don't want to tempt fate, but I think . . . I pray . . . I think . . . I hope, oh God, I think, think, only think – Andy still likes me. I meant to thank him for the birthday card but I was struck dumb with gratitude at his compliment. Probably just as well, because if the powers of speech had returned I'd probably have invited him to move in with me, instead of round for a drink on Boxing Day, which is what I wanted to say.

25 December

Decided to be very grown up and rang Mum to wish her happy Christmas, she was very nice and sweet! Keith obviously hasn't told her Dad's glad tidings.

26 December

Never going home again for Christmas, had a riot with Old Mrs M. yesterday. As a big treat, I let her watch the *Street* special after all. We were both quite tiddly by the time it came on, so I didn't care anyway (the never-touching-alcohol-again promise will only apply in the New Year and only when absolutely necessary). She really is good company, very open-minded. I hope I'm like her when I'm that old, except not housebound obviously, or deaf, or addicted to *Coronation Street* actually, but like her in other ways.

Sat around most of this evening with her too – it's great just doing what I want, eating and drinking what I want in front of someone who doesn't care – mustn't keep this level of consumption up for the entire season, though, or I won't be able to get out of her flat.

NB: I wonder if the Samaritans take calls from people who've eaten too much . . . well, they did write to me, after all, they must have thought I might need their number for a reason.

27 December

Andy's just rung! He wants to pop round for a drink . . . HELP, I haven't washed my hair for the last two days . . . I'd look a bit silly wearing a hat in the house . . . unless I said I'd just come in, but then I can't have done because he's just phoned and I was in, so obviously I can't have *just* come in . . . oh, does it matter?

28 December

Jingle bells, jingle bells, jingle all the way. Santa came to town, well, in the shape of Andy. He came round last night, we chatted and everything and then conversation got round to Carlo, turns out Andy knew all the time that Carlo wasn't gay! Poor Andy, he thought I'd dumped him for Carlo – I don't know where he got that idea, as I remember Andy dumped me, well, made it plain he'd lost interest. That's my recollection; anyway, I suppose it doesn't really matter any more. It seems he was quite upset, he said he'd taken the Edinburgh transfer so that he wouldn't have to see me every day (that was because he was upset rather than not wanting to see me every day for any other reason, I think). Anyway, after a while he said he missed me and wanted to be with me and did I feel the same!! I was completely taken aback, and so pleased half of me was doing somersaults inside and the other half was desperate to get on the phone to Sally and ask her what she thought. I didn't think that would be very sensitive to Andy, though – well, not while he was still there . . . in the room.

29 December

You will never guess what I've been doing. I have spent the last two days lying around in bed with Andy. Me, lying around in bed chatting. Well, there has been some sex, obviously, but I didn't panic once about being naked, I haven't kept my pyjamas and vest on, and one time we even did it with the lights on! Admittedly I was lying down, but still. The most amazing thing of all, though, happened yesterday in the middle of the day – we were lying in bed having a really nice time and then I realised I needed to pee and I got up to go to the loo without thinking about it! I only had a T-shirt on and it didn't cover my bum but I got up to go to the loo without thinking about it, without worrying (well, not a lot) what Andy would think! Actually, thinking about it now, what had happened the night before had probably given me the confidence to do that. I'd got up in the night to pee and thought he was asleep but he wasn't and he turned the light on when I was in the middle of reaching for my dressing gown (the newish one) and somehow instead of doing what I would normally, instinctively have done, which is swiftly drop to the floor, pressing myself into the carpet like a commando trying to get under some barbed wire until he went back to sleep, I managed to stay standing there, with the light on – nude, until I'd got the dressing gown on! I admit I was holding my stomach in and not breathing and it was only for a nanosecond and he was half asleep – but the great thing is I have stood up in front of someone in the nude and he still likes me!

I've got to go into work tomorrow, Andy is going to wait for me here – sweet. It's really great having him around (although it is quite annoying when he doesn't put the milk back properly on the right shelf in the fridge . . . but I do like him).

30 December

Popped into work quickly, no one else was around, officially we're closed until the 2nd. I just wanted to finish off that chart properly in case Keen John appears on the 2nd with a state-of-the-art version he's spent the whole of Christmas preparing.

Took Andy over to see Old Mrs M., I think she liked him, she was positively flirting with him, he was very kind and nice to her.

NB: It would be really mad to think he fancied her ... wouldn't it?

NNB: Saw Foghorn on my way out this morning, I'm sure she gave me a really approving look when she said hello. Like, having got a boyfriend (she must have seen Andy) I've now become a superior being, like her. I always knew people with boyfriends thought they were members of some special élite club. Briefly toyed with the idea of chucking Andy just to show her but then realised that would be sort of cutting off my nose to spite my face.

31 December

Another amazing thing has happened! When I got back from work today (had to go in this morning too), Andy had bought some crisps and nuts and stuff and put them out in bowls (Sally and Lovely Dan are coming round tonight, before we go off to some friend of Dan's party). Anyway, after I'd changed, I came back into the living room and he'd poured some drinks, handed me a glass and then offered me the bowl full of nuts. Instinctively my body went rigid, I looked at the nuts and then at him to see if he was trying to catch me out, you know, waiting for me to take a handful and then say, 'Do you really think you should be eating those?' I stood frozen to the spot for a moment but then thought this might be the only way to find out if he was going to turn out to be like Perfect Peter, so I closed my eyes, took a deep breath and picked up a handful! It wasn't a test! It wasn't a test! He didn't do anything, he didn't say anything, he just put the bowl back on the sideboard, just like that, I can't believe how happy I felt. I even ate the nuts, I felt so brilliant. Andy is the most fantastic man on earth! Gosh, this all feels like an out-of-body experience, when is it all going to end?

The info about the women's group had arrived at work today, I'm very excited about all of this. I've made my mind up, if it's the last thing I ever do, I'm going to do my best to help create a world where it's safe to have a big bum.